COLIN CALLS THE HELP DESK

An Irreverent Tale of Corporate Life

Elwood Scott

Published by: Roadhouse Publications

Illustrations by Mitch Pleasance Tattoo Artist.
Instagram: @mitchpleasance
Written by: Elwood Scott. Twitter: @e_scottauthor.
Instagram: @e_scott_author
First edition 2023. Melbourne Australia.

ISBN: 978-0-6450524-2-8

Dedication

Colin Calls the Help Desk is dedicated to everyone (whether in an office or not) who works hard, strives to do their best, and still manages to get their job done each day...

Despite the ongoing 'support' of their bosses, co-workers, and the business systems, procedures and processes put in place to assist them.

And to Ben, Sally and Parker.

Contents

A Colin the Koala FAQ

Below you will find answers to the most common
questions you may have about
COLIN CALLS THE HELP DESK

Q. The main character is called Colin the Koala. Is -
The Koala - a nickname? Like Jimmy the Finch,
Nikki the Llama or Oblong Doug?
A. Nope. Colin the Koala is actually a Koala.

Q. But aren't koalas generally naked, drunk and
spend all their time sleeping or catching Chlamydia?
A. No, you're thinking of Bryan from Accounting.
Colin wears a suit, is sober, a little naive and excited to
lean-in, add value and grab the low hanging fruit.

Q. Okay. So, if there's a koala in the office, there must
be other animals as well.
A. That's technically more of a statement than a
question, but no there isn't. Colin is the only animal in
the office.

Q. Right. I think I've got it now. The story revolves
around everyone's confusion that there's a koala
working in their office.
A. Also not a question and no. No-one (with the
exception of a douche-canoe in Book Two who asks
Colin if he's a diversity hire) pays any attention to it.

Q. I recognise most of the people in this book. Did
you get your ideas from my workplace?
A. No. My lawyer tells me they are all fictional.

Q. Did you go to University to become a writer?
A. No. I don't have any formal writing koala-fications.

The New Starter

Colin the Koala gazes out of the bus window into the perfect sunny Monday morning. He grabs the handrail to stop sliding off the seat as the driver slams on the brakes to avoid running through an unexpected pedestrian crossing.

Colin smiles at the nice lady sitting in the seat next to him. "Ooh. What type of leaf is that you're chewing?" he asks politely.

She turns her head slowly and takes a large bite from the empty paper cup in her hand.

"Oh," Colin says and snatches the handrail again as the bus snaps forward. "It's my first day in my new job today. I'm so excited about having my own desk, with a new computer full of all the latest software, and working as part of a crack team – all supporting each other," he bubbles. "There's my building!" he turns and points excitedly.

The bus suddenly swerves into the bus stop and the driver's thick glasses slip down to the end of his nose as he jerks to a halt. He ignores the horns blaring around him, and grunts once before pushing them back up again.

"This is my stop," Colin stands up to join the queue of passengers getting off. "I can't wait to 'knuckle-down' and work hard to help my teammates achieve our goals and contribute to the success of the company."

When the lady next to him doesn't move, Colin points past her to the aisle. "Um. Sorry. I just need to..." he smiles again.

She takes another bite of the cup and moves her legs almost imperceptibly to one side, giving just enough room to uncomfortably squeeze through.

"Thanks!" Colin scootches past. "I hope you have as much fun today as I will," he calls out over his shoulder as he scurries to the exit.

He checks his watch as he gets to the door. "Thank you for getting me to work on schedule," he says to the driver as he steps onto the footpath. "It's my first day in my new job today and—"

The driver pulls a lever and the doors hiss and slam closed. The bus engine roars and the driver jerks into traffic to a cacophony of horns and shouts. He wanders between lanes while he tries to catch the glasses falling into his lap.

Colin waves goodbye and strides jauntily toward the big office building, a screech of tyres and car horns ringing out behind him.

Colin has only been to the city twice before. Once on a school excursion to the museum. The second for an awkward doctor's visit the time he had eaten too much cheese.

Today though, he's very excited to be here to start his new job.

Last night he had made sure to lay out his suit and tie, set two alarms (and later; a supplementary, third, back-up alarm) and map out his trip to make sure he would arrive early.

But not too early.

"Right on schedule," he smiles proudly as he steps up to the front of the huge office building. "This is so cool!"

He stares up at the old heritage style entranceway, full of broad brick arches and rough finishes, friendly earthy brown tones and olde-world charm and smiles broadly. "You're on your way Mr. Koala," he says and steps through the main door to the lobby.

Suddenly everything switches to a huge, imposing areas full of bright glaring glass, obtuse angles and polished aluminium. "Gosh," Colin flicks his head from side to side.

He sucks in a breath, steps back out again to check he hadn't somehow walked through the wrong door and feels a little bit like he's stumbled into a Black Mirror episode.

He gawks at the tide of people making their way towards the entrance. "Everyone seems so busy and important," he says, quickly stepping out of the way of a tall man balancing three coffees. "I can't wait to join in and be busy and important too."

Colin puffs out his chest to look busy and important

and realises that he's being swept slowly across the lobby towards the main entrance and the security gates.

He worries for a moment, then remembers what Mr Platypus had told the class in school if they ever found themselves getting pulled along in the river.

"Go with the flow, and swim diagonally to the side."

Colin slips sideways, navigates his way to the edge and moves safely off to the side and pulls out the Special Reminder Notebook he had bought just for his new job. He had written: 'Colin's Special Reminder Notebook - Please do not steal' and added a drawing of a smiley face across the front, in his neatest handwriting.

He checks his first day instructions (even though he knows them by heart). His friends, who already worked hard in their own jobs, had given him some tips. He'd made sure to take note that it was important to 'Suck-up-to-the-Boss.' But not enough to be a 'Brown-Nose'.

Colin wasn't sure why the colour of his nose would make a difference, but he had made sure to check in the mirror before he left home this morning and had been relieved to discover that, as always, it was still black. He reads the page with his first instruction for the day:

Go to the Security Desk and have my picture taken for an Entry Pass.

He scurries over and joins the queue for the Security desk behind a very tall man in jeans and a plaid shirt. "Hi!" says Colin. "My name's Colin. It's my first day today. Is this your first day too?" he cranes neck upwards. "Maybe we could be first day buddies."

When the man turns around to answer, Colin's eyes open wide. He has a scruffy beard so long that it reaches all the way to his belt buckle.

Colin quickly stuffs his paws in his pockets to actively resist an urge to climb up it.

"Yeah, na," the bearded man says, scratching his cheek. "Forgot my pass. Have to get a Badge of Shame," he says with a booming voice, and laughs.

Colin frowns and remembers the time his friend Archie the kelpie had gone to the animal hospital, and had come home with a *cone* of shame, and gulps. He hopes he doesn't ever forget *his* pass.

The man with the giant beard takes his temporary pass from the security guard and wishes Colin luck for his first day.

Colin's steps forward and waits politely at the counter for a few moments, then realises the security guard maybe can't see him all the way down on the floor, and climbs up onto the desk.

"Hi!" he declares with a big smile as he pops up onto the counter.

"Jesus!" the guard jumps and drops her phone onto the floor. "Where did you come from?"

Colin giggles. "I came from home," he says and scratches his head. "And I think you've confused me with someone else. *My* name is Colin. I'm starting today and my first job is to get my picture taken for my very own Entry Pass."

The Security Guard takes a few deep breaths to return her heart rate to normal, and picks up her phone off the floor. She asks for Colin's paperwork and checks it against her computer, in between replying to text messages and snarling at her phone.

She tells Colin to stand against the wall in front of the camera and get ready to have his picture taken.

Colin stands in front of the special security photo background but he only just reaches the bottom of the screen. "I'm not sure I'm tall enou—"

"Ready?" the security guard asks, shaking her head angrily at her phone and typing another reply.

"Maybe can I get a chair?" Colin stands on his tip-toes. "I don't know if—"

"Three, two, one."

POP! Goes the fur on the top of Colin's head.

Click! Goes the camera.

The Security Guard tells Colin he will need to come back tomorrow and collect his pass; and that she'll give him a special pass for today.

Colin glances over to where the man with the beard had gone with his Badge of Shame and feels his heart beat faster as the security guard slides the pass over the counter face down.

He holds his breath and turns it over slowly... "Phew," he puffs. It doesn't say 'Badge of Shame', it just says 'Temporary Pass'.

Or it would, if someone hadn't scratched off the 'P'. So instead, it reads, 'Temporary ass.'

"I need to meet my new Boss, Bob," Colin smiles and checks his notes again. "My Instructions say to ask you to call him."

The security guard tells Colin that's not her job and

to go to the Reception counter.

"Okay," Colin nods. "Where would I find the—" he tries to ask, but the security guard is already busy angrily typing another text message.

Colin climbs up onto one of the shelves the way he would a tree in the bush, and peers around the big open area until he spies a sign that reads - Reception. He slips back into the river of people and lets it carry him to the Reception counter.

He tells the man at the desk it's his first day, and that he's there to meet his new Boss; Bob. And that Bob would come down to meet him and show him around the office and introduce him to his new team.

The man forces a fake smile and dials Bob the Boss' number. He stares blankly at nothing and chews loudly while he waits for an answer.

Colin checks his watch and smiles. Four minutes to nine. Right on time. A little early... but not too early. He gives himself a tiny paw pump.

"This is so exciting. Look at how busy everyone is, ready to work hard to get the job done," Colin says watching the people streaming into the office. Some are grumbling. Others laughing. One man slaps his pass loudly several times on the automatic gate when it doesn't open the first time.

"Yeah, there's no answer," the man says chewing loudly. "Who else you supposed to meet?"

Colin wonders what type of leaf he's chewing as he checks his notes again. "Randall," he smiles looking up. "Randall is my 'Buddy.'"

After a brief unresolved discussion of whether Randall is a first, or last, name, the man chews more quickly; writes an email to Bob, and includes a couple of other people at random who look like they work on the same floor.

"You can wait over there," he says without pointing anywhere.

Colin checks his watch. Ten past nine. "I guess Bob must be busy in an important meeting."

"Yeah, sure," the man shrugs and stares off into the middle distance again.

On the 19th floor, Bob the Boss hitches up his pants and flushes the toilet. He wets his hands in the closest sink, but when he pumps the lever for soap; nothing comes out.

He tries the next one. Also empty.

He shakes his wet hands and looks glumly at the empty paper-towel dispenser. He waves his hands under the automatic dryer - which gives one vague puff. He waves his hands under the sensor again like he's conducting an orchestra while having a seizure.

It eventually gives two more soft sputters and pumps out less air than a summer breeze. "I can't believe they still haven't fixed that," he grumbles and wipes his wet hands on the back of his pants. He pulls open the door back to the corridor, ignoring the sign that reads – 'Report any problems with this facility to have them promptly repaired', and can't shake a niggling feeling in the back of his head that he's forgotten something, and asks Gina whether she knows what he's forgotten.

"I'm not your PA, how would I know?" she mumbles under her breath. Then without looking up says. "I got a message there's a Koala in Reception?"

"Shit!" Bob slaps his palm on his forehead, leaving a tiny damp spot. He rushes to the elevators; past the empty desk he had set aside for his new starter. He stops suddenly and realises he has forgotten to organise a computer.

He stares at the ceiling for a few seconds, takes four deep breaths, then turns back to ask Gina. He knows Gina will help, because she respects him as a leader.

"Could you call I.T. and sort out a new computer while I run down to reception?" he turns back towards the lifts.

"Sure," Gina says and glares into his back. "Even though your crap communication skills and lack of planning aren't my responsibility," she mumbles quietly.

"Thanks Gina!" Bob calls over his shoulder. "I really appreciate it," he yells, even though he knows, that she knows, he doesn't.

"No problems at all," Gina calls back cheerily and sticks up her middle finger at his rapidly disappearing back. "And you've got wet handprints on your arse," she says and dials the number for I.T.

Colin sits, swinging his tiny legs back and forth on the uncomfortable, but fashion-designed chair, keeping a keen eye out for anyone who might look like a 'Bob'.

Whenever someone who looks like a Bob appears, Colin sits up straight, smiles eagerly, and gets ready to push himself off the chair, ready to make a good first impression.

When none turn out to be a Bob, he starts counting how many times he swings his legs.

"87. 88. 89," he whispers quietly to himself when a man who doesn't look anything at all like a Bob, rushes up to Reception.

"There's... puff puff... a Koala here somewhere?"

The man behind the desk chews loudly and points vaguely in Colin's direction.

Bob spins around, straightens himself up and walks confidently over. "HI!" he says holding his hand out. "Sorry for being late," he shakes Colin's paw, and says he had been in a special important meeting. Bob says how pleased he is to have Colin starting today. That there is a lot to do. And a Koala like Colin is exactly the right marsupial for the job.

Colin is pleased that Bob the Boss is already excited

to have him working there. He follows Bob to the elevator, wiping his unexpectedly damp paw on his jacket.

As they head upstairs in the lift Bob tells Colin all about how well the team works together since he had taken over as their leader. "Teamwork is important," Bob says, "and good leadership is essential to great teamwork." He pokes the air with his finger for emphasis.

Colin nods. "Yes, I've heard that—"

"I should really be in a more senior role by now," Bob pretends to laugh as though he's not frustrated about it. "But I'm a victim of my own success. I'm such a good leader," he shrugs, "they can't *afford* to promote me," he says and rushes out of the lift.

Colin moves his little legs quickly to try and keep up with his fast-walking Boss, while trying to take in the exciting new environment. They walk past a poster that reads – 'Contact your Union Representative! Don't let Management push you around.'

Colin makes a note in his head to ask who this Management person is, and why they like to push people. Mrs Wombat, his kindergarten teacher had always been unwavering with her rules: 'No poking. No biting. No pushing.'

"I don't know, maybe I'm just destined to be a Team Leader all my life..." Bob continues and sighs. "What does it matter anyway? No-one cares... Here's your desk!" Bob says suddenly pointing to a desk. There's several coffee marks, an odd stain where something has been spilt and left to dry and the handle to raise and lower it seems to be missing.

In front of a computer monitor that hangs at an angle that no one would choose on purpose, is a hastily written sign.

It says: 'Welcome!'

It doesn't say 'Welcome *Colin*,' because when Gina had called George (who looks after the Social Club and had written the sign) to tell him they had a new starter, she didn't know Colin's name.

"This is the new team member we've been waiting for," Bob declares to Gina. "He's starting today."

"I know," Gina pulls her lips back in what Colin thinks is supposed to be a smile at Bob but looks more like a grimace. "I just organised his computer, because you hadn—"

Welcome!" Bob calls again and quickly holds the sign high, as though he was the one responsible for it.

Colin stares past him at the empty desk. "Is *that*... my desk?" Colin asks, eyes wide.

"Uh. Yes. Is it alright for your, um... needs?" Bob looks around at Gina. "I can have it changed. Gina really should have made sure it was wiped clean at least before—"

"Me?"

Colin stares at the desk then back to Bob. "It's exactly the way I had dreamt it would be," he takes a deep breath. "There's a phone. Two monitors," he steps forward and spins the chair. "And a big adjustable chair."

"Your eyes are a little watery," Bob says leaning towards him. "Is that the air conditioning? Do I need to get Gina to fix the air conditioning?"

Colin rubs his nose and smiles. "It's perfect," he sniffs and steps back. "I can't wait to get started. Thank you!" he smiles at Gina.

"I was the one who told her to organise it," Bob says hastily.

Colin looks at the desk in awe. "There's so much

room," he shakes his head slowly. "it's bigger than my first tree. Is it *all* mine?"

"It sure is," Bob smiles and pats Colin inappropriately on the back.

"Yeah," Gina snorts. "It's all yours..." she glances over at Bob. "*Most* of the time. Human Resources just introduced 'flexible desking'—"

"Thank you, Gina," Bob says quickly. "Let's let Colin get settled in."

"So it's all yours," she ignores him and continues, "except for when maybe 'Management' wants to use it," she makes air quotes.

Colin wonders if that's why this Management person pushes people. To sit at their desk. All Management would need to do is ask, Colin thinks looking at the big open space. This desk is big enough for both of them.

"Or," a nice lady who introduces herself as Pooja jumps in, "if someone happens to arrive earlier than you in the morning and decides to sit there..." she thinks for a moment. "Or there's other people from outside our team who sit there because Human Resources haven't allocated enough desks to go around in their area and they don't want to sit at the rickety kitchen tables that HR have started pretending were *always* designed for people to sit at as permanent desks, when they clearly aren't—"

"Okay. Thank you," Bob interrupts gruffly. "I think Colin gets the idea," he smiles. "It's still in the transition stages," he declares and shifts awkwardly from one foot to the other. "Look at this chair!" Bob pulls it out for him, fiddling with the handles. "You can move all these levers to adjust it."

He grabs an instruction pamphlet with half the front page missing from another desk. "Here's the instructions on how to set yourself up perfectly ergonomically," he reads from the front cover.

Colin climbs up onto the chair and bounces a couple of times. He adjusts the chair this way and that, unsuccessfully attempting to get comfortable. One of the levers doesn't work, so the seat pan is stuck in a permanent tilt, causing him to slide slowly forward. "Maybe I'll finish that up later," he says, realising everyone is staring at him trying to get the right setup at a desk designed for an 'average' employee.

"Looks like you're good to go," Bob claps his

hands. "Make sure to complete your compulsory on-line training courses: 'Your Health and Safety are our number one priority' and 'Our people are our greatest asset'."

"Okey dokey." Colin gives Bob a crisp salute. "I'm looking forward to getting some new..." he smiles, trying to hold back a laugh, but can't help himself and giggles. "Koala-fications."

Bob frowns. "No, they're only in-house courses, so there's no certificates or anything."

"I know, I was just making a—"

"Yeah," Bob says. "If you can get straight onto that. Otherwise I'll have Human Resources on my back," he snorts, "and we'll both get a *million* reminder emails," he stares off vaguely into the middle distance. "Again..."

Colin is about to say - "That's a lot of emails," when a man with a brown bow tie, carrying a pile of papers walks up behind Bob and Gina.

"Oh, and whatever you do, don't forget - 'Ethics are Essential,'" Gina shakes her head and laughs. "Where you get to learn all about how to be ethical when other companies shower you with gifts and junkets to get you to use their products or services."

"Oh. I didn't know we needed to deal with outside companies," Colin says excitedly.

"We don't," Gina replies flatly.

"Oh yeah, that one," Bob rolls his eyes. "It's pointless. Just ask Vanessa to give you a copy of the answers."

Colin scribbles it down in his Special Reminder notebook:

Ask Vanessa for the answers to the Ethics training.

"Got it."

"I assume this is the new starter?" the man in the brown bow tie asks standing behind Bob.

Bob's eyes pop wide open. There's an awkward silence, before he clears his throat and smiles. "Ahem. Colin. This is Arthur. From, ah... Human Resources."

"Hello," Arthur says in a way that implies he's not quite sure why he needs to. "I look after the mandatory training courses Bob was helpfully advising you of," he glares at Bob. "As well as onboarding." He drops half the stack of papers he's holding on Colin's desk without looking at him. "This is your tax declaration, your social club application, bike locker request form, map of the building." He starts another pile. "You'll need to sign and date these, have them witnessed and provide copies to your Manager, Human Resources and Employment Services..."

Colin watches Arthur drop the remainder of the forms onto his new desk, each one landing slightly more out of kilter on top of the previous one, creating an increasingly wobbly stack. Colin desperately wants to reach forward and straighten them; but is worried Arthur might just keep dropping his papers, and Colin would become part of the pile.

"...our health and safety rules, consent for drug and alcohol testing, confidentiality agreement, regulations on phone etiquette, emergency evacuation response, use of electronics, and the list of actions that will result in termination of employment," he smiles. "And of course, you'll need to acknowledge you have read, understood and agree to be bound by the terms and conditions of our employee booklet."

He drops a final stack of paper with the cover page: 'We empower you to be your best!' onto the pile, causing it to lean precariously to the left.

Arthur steps back and folds his arms. "You'll need to complete and return them ASAP," he says crisply, saying 'asap' as a word, not an acronym.

Colin looks at the pile almost as high as he is, and at Arthur. He wants to ask if his bow tie lights up and spins, the way Old Mr Emu's would sometimes, but decides it's best not to. "Uhh, okay. ASAP," he says, also saying it as a word.

"One final item," Arthur smiles and hands Colin a small parcel wrapped in brown paper. "Here's your nameplate. It's simpler for people to find you when you are flexible desking."

"Not simpler than knowing where someone always sits," Gina mumbles.

Colin grins from ear to ear. A nameplate! "I've hit the big time!" he says bouncing on the chair, causing him to slide forward again.

Even though he's almost bursting, he knows it's important not to just rip the wrapping off presents, so he says thank you, carefully unwraps the nameplate and places it down on the desk for them all to see.

Bob points to it. "Collinn," he frowns. "Funny way to spell it," and tilts his head. "Is that a Koala thing?"

"Uh... no," Colin rubs his neck. "There's actually only one 'L' and there should only be one 'N' at the end."

"Oh. Sorry," Arthur says, clearly indicating he isn't. "Where does the other 'N' go?"

Bob grabs a post-it note and writes N in the middle of it, ready to place it in the right spot.

"Um. There's only *one* N," Colin smiles, "and one L in the middle."

"Right," Bob says writing L on another post-it note. "Where does the other 'L' go?" Bob says sticking the 'N' post-it onto the nameplate to cover up the second N, making it read: 'Colli N'.

"You must be the new guy," a deep voice causes Colin to jump.

He looks up at a huge man who introduces himself as George, the President of the social club. George looks like he could snap a eucalyptus tree in two with his bare hands. Even his hands have muscles. George glances at the nameplate and holds out his hand to shake. "I've never seen a name spelt that way before," he says. "Is that a Koala thing?"

"No, it's not a Koala thing—" Colin says his paw

disappearing into George's giant hand.

"Anyway, it's nice to meet you," he reads the nameplate, "Collie N," and smiles.

"It's actually just Colin—"

"If you need anything," Arthur smiles cutting in, "don't hesitate to speak to your Buddy," he turns to back Bob. "Who's his Buddy?"

"Randall," Colin says helpfully.

"Okay," nods Arthur. "Can you chase up Randall and tell him his new starter Collie N is here?" he looks at Bob.

"It's Colin," Colin says helpfully.

"Poor form for Randall not to be here with the new starter already," Arthur shakes his head and disappears back down the corridor towards the lifts.

"Randall?" George goes to scratch his head, but because his biceps are so big, he needs to tilt his head sideways to be able to reach.

"Randall?" Gina looks at George blankly.

"Alrighty," Bob rubs his hands together and checks the time. "I'll leave you to get down to it. I've got lots of important work I need to do. Your buddy... Merebnbnner," he mumbles to cover the fact he wasn't paying attention and doesn't know the buddy's name, "will walk you through your job expectations and tasks, give you a tour of the building, and set you up so you can get started on doing some proper work," he says and pats Colin on the shoulder before walking off toward his desk.

Colin assures Bob the Boss he will get right onto it and that he can't wait to be productive! "I'll complete my compulsory on-line training courses while I'm waiting for my computer."

Bob stops and turns around. "Yes. Well, if Gina had organised your computer on time..." he mutters under his breath.

"*Really?*" Gina folds her arms and raises an eyebrow at Bob.

Bob smiles awkwardly and heads off toward the lift. "If you could just—"

"Sure, why don't *I* follow that up again then," she glares at him.

"I've got an important meeting to get to," he says, not knowing Gina, Vanessa and George know that he's actually sneaking to the cafe for a donut by himself, so he doesn't have to bring back some for the others.

Colin looks over at the paper Arthur has left on the desk for him. "Perhaps I'll promptly proceed with this precarious pile of papers," he says, smiling at his alliteration.

"I'll call I.T. again about your lack of laptop," Gina heads back to her desk.

The others re-iterate their welcomes, wish him luck and wander back to their respective desks.

Colin adjusts his chair again, creating a slightly less forward angle and starts work on the huge pile of forms.

He places the fifth handwritten form that required exactly the same information as the previous forms onto his 'Complete' pile and wonders why they don't just put the onboarding forms online, so you only need to fill in the same details once.

After nearly an hour, he places the final form squarely on top of his 'Complete' pile.

"Done," he calls to Gina, who's staring at her screen. He smiles briefly at her. "Looking forward to my new computer," he says and waits.

After a few minutes without a response, he waves tentatively.

When Gina eventually notices him, she looks over without removing her earphones and says, "YOUR COMPUTER IS GOING TO BE A WHILE. WHY DON'T YOU MAYBE GET A COFFEE OR SOMETHING."

He flinches. "Okay," he says looking around. "I can do that. Where's the coffee room?" he looks back at Gina, but she's back to her screen.

"Thank... you..." Colin mouths to her. "Sorry, it looks like you're very busy," he says, unable to see that she's taking a quiz to find out what colour her spirit animal's aura is. "I'll find it," he nods once. "How hard can it be to find coffee?" He slides down off the chair and makes one final check that the paper pile isn't going to collapse. He clears his throat and says as professionally as he can muster. "Oh, and if Randall stops by looking for me, could you please let him know I'm just grabbing a coffee and should be back soon."

But when he turns around to check Gina has heard him, her desk is empty.

He looks from her empty chair back to his own empty desk and his tiny shoulders slump a little. "This isn't what I was anticipating my first day to be at all," frowns. By now he was expecting to be 'nailing his KPIs' (even though he wasn't sure exactly what that meant, but his friends had all agreed it was important) and collaborating.

He sniffs the air. "I think coffee is that way," he points along the corridor. "Let's get those wagon trains a' movin'," he says in his best cowboy voice and waves his arm.

He sets of along the corridor, past the half full photocopy paper boxes and comes to an intersection. He uses his - any time I'm unsure which direction to go: go left – rule. He turns down the corridor and sees a lady rushing towards him.

"Hi," Colin waves at her, "it's my first day, and because I'm new I don't know where anything is. Can you help me find where we keep the coffee?"

The lady stops so suddenly Colin is expecting to hear a squeal of brakes.

She glares down at him. "Excuse me?" she says very quickly. "I'm very busy."

"Hi!" Colin says again, holding out his paw to shake. "I'm Colin. I'm new. I need to grab a coffee.

Could you tell me where the kitchen is please?" he looks at her security pass and sees her name is Brenda. "Would you like to grab a coffee with me?" he looks up at her and lifts his eyebrows hopefully. "It would be nice to have a new friend at work."

"It must be wonderful to have time for coffee," Brenda thrusts her hands on her hips. "I'm so busy I don't have time to scratch myself."

Colin smiles and wonders if it would be inappropriate to offer to help with her itch. His claws are very good for scratching. But before he can say anything she starts waving vaguely in the direction he is heading.

Colin listens politely as Brenda spends ten minutes complaining about her how overloaded with work she is and how she 'has to do everything around here'.

"Um, you were telling me where the kitchen is?" Colin jumps in when she finally takes a breath.

"The kitchen's down there, left and then right. Turn right into the corridor three meeting rooms before the big one. I don't have time to walk you down there. You wouldn't believe how much work they give me."

"I'll tell you..." she says still talking as she storms off.

"Um... Thank you!" Colin calls out, but Brenda doesn't hear because she is already busy telling Gina about how overloaded with work she is.

Colin looks up and down the corridor, squinting in the direction Brenda pointed and continues on. He spends a few minutes of walking in circles and wondering how to know which is the right corridor if it's *before* the big meeting room...

"You right mate?" a balding man asks, stuffing his white shirt into his trousers as he walks over. "You look a bit lost," he says. "But not in the way most people who work here do!" He laughs loudly and his shirt pulls up out of his trousers again.

Colin doesn't really understand why it's funny that the people who work here get lost, but it makes him feel a little better about his situation.

Colin introduces himself and explains that it's his first day.

"Sorry to hear that," he laughs. "Graham," he says and shakes Colin's paw. "What are you doing down this end?"

Colin explains he's waiting for his computer to arrive so he can start his work and in the meantime, he's looking for the kitchen to get a coffee.

"Oh Christ no!" Graham exclaims.

Colin gulps. "But, um, Gina said—"

"No, you don't want that rubbish they've got here." Graham shakes his head intensely.

Colin relaxes, and shakes his head too, even though he's not sure why. He doesn't mind instant coffee. But it's best to be polite.

"You're in luck," Graham says and holds up a plastic re-useable coffee cup. "I'm heading out now. Come along, I'll introduce you to the coffee shop across the road."

Colin looks at the cup and notices it says: 'The beatings will continue until morale improves', and makes sure to smiles broadly to show his morale is high. Just in case.

"Okay, thanks," says Colin as they step into the lift. "I hope Randall won't be looking for me," he ponders for a moment, then adds. "Randall's my Buddy. He's going to give me the tour and tell me all about my job."

"Who's Randall?" Graham asks as they walk to the front exit doors to the street.

"I don't know," Colin shrugs. "I haven't met him yet. Have you worked here long?"

Graham tells Colin he's worked for the company for more than twenty years. "Place wouldn't survive without me," he says.

Colin is excited to meet someone so essential on his first day! "Twenty years!" Colin gasps as they cross the road. "You must really love it here."

Graham laughs. "Ha!. Na, I'm just hanging out for redundancy," he adds.

Colin doesn't want to seem silly for not knowing what a 'redundancy' is, but decides they must be very important if the company wouldn't survive without Graham around to hang them out.

"Anyway, if you need to know anything, come see me," Graham winks. "I know where all the bodies are buried."

Colin frowns and decides it's best not to ask why the company buries bodies.

"Here's the place," Graham says holding the cafe door open.

Colin looks over at the big wooden counter, and the chalkboard that reads: 'Special House Blend - Venezuelan Beaver Coffee. Notes of wood-chips, organic aluminium and blue cheese over slow-cooked rice.'

He represses a shudder and hopes they just have some normal coffee.

Graham hands over his re-usable cup to the man in the leather apron with the man-bun behind the counter. "Workin' hard or hardly workin'?" he laughs.

It must be too noisy for the coffee man to hear over the sound of the machine, thinks Colin, because he doesn't answer Graham's question.

Colin lifts himself up on the counter and orders his favourite coffee – A cappuccino with double chocolate on top, and promises to buy a re-usable cup for next time.

"Name?" the barista asks, pen poised.

"It's Colin," Colin says and points at his new friend, "I work with Graham," he smiles broadly.

"Okay," the barista says disinterestedly, and

scribbles the name on the cup.

Colin steps back with Graham so the next people can place their orders. While they are waiting, Graham helps Colin to understand the company, how it runs and who's important. He starts by telling him all the things he's been pointing out over the years that are either broken, impractical, or plain stupid, and that are dragging the company down.

Colin nods knowingly. "Yes. I know what you mean. Mrs. Wombat would always say – 'Be on the look-out for ways we can help improve our environment'," he smiles broadly. "I'm interested to know more about ways to make the company better. Tell me about all the things you've helped fix Graham."

"Fix?" Graham snorts. "Yeah. Not *my* job mate."

"Coffee for Callen!" the barista yells to the waiting group.

Colin looks around. He's surprised that his coffee wasn't ready before the other people's. When no-one steps forward, he says, "Colin?" and stands on his tiptoes expectantly.

The Barista turns the cup to show where he has

written Callen. "Cappuccino. Extra chocolate."

Colin looks around at the people waiting. No-one looks like a Callen, he thinks. He waits a few moments more, and no Callens are coming forward. "Uh. That *sounds* like mine..." he leans forward. "But could it be Colin?"

He checks again. "Says Callen," he shrugs and hands the cup to him. "Have a good one Callen," the barista calls as Graham opens the door back to the street.

"You get that much?" Graham asks. "The *Callen* thing?"

"Not really," Colin replies with a shrug.

"Huh. I would have thought *Colin* was pretty straightforward," Graham says taking a sip of his coffee. "Ahh. Better than that crap you would have got in the kitchen."

"Yes, it is. I think..." Colin nods politely, noticing the hint of organic aluminium after-taste. As they walk back, he thanks Graham for giving him the low-down, and telling him 'How it really is'.

Graham promises to fill him in on 'who's who in the zoo' and waves goodbye as the exit the lifts and head back to their desks.

❧

"I just had coffee with Graham," Colin says raising his cup to Gina as he walks back to his desk.

"In the middle of something," Gina says without looking up at him.

"Sorry," Colin says. "Have you heard from Randall by any chance?" he asks quickly.

"Haven't heard from anyone by that name," Gina says glancing over and noticing Colin's cup. "I thought your name was Colin?" she says.

"Ha," Colin laughs, "It is. Graham took me to the coffee shop across the road, and he just got my name wrong. Doesn't matter."

Gina suddenly sits up in chair, as though someone has switched her on. "No," she says. "No, it does matter," she points her finger at Colin. "That barista. You have to watch him. Only half pays attention, then tells *me*," her voice rises as she taps her chest, "that *I* made a mistake with the order."

"Okay..." Colin says.

"I know what I ordered pal," she grunts. "It was always *my* fault when something was wrong..."

"Ah..." Colin shifts awkwardly. "Thank you," he takes a step backwards. "I'll make sure I'm more careful when I order in future. I'm sorry to hear about... your coffee order..." he tries to smile sympathetically.

"Thanks," she says, not looking at him.

"Anyway, it's not *your* fault. I wouldn't go there. But if you do," Colin notices Gina's face soften, for just a moment. "Don't let him push you around." Then slip back to its usual half scowl.

'Push me around?' Colin thinks, 'Is he *Management?*'

"Oh yeah. You've got a present," Gina waves disinterestedly at Colin's desk.

Colin looks over and his shoulder and notices a thin black item on his desk. "Is that?" he says softly, his eyes widening. He moves closer, looking between it and Gina. "Is that my..." he looks around excitedly, "my... new computer..." and rushes up to his desk. "It is!" he clenches his paw and fist pumps the air.

"Gina!" he calls back to her over his shoulder. "My

brand-new computer is here!" He climbs up excitedly up onto his chair, slides forward, pushes himself back and slides forward again. "Ha ha," he laughs pointing. "Did you put these funny stickers on it for me," he says pulling it closer. He runs a claw slowly across the top as though he's Indiana Jones opening a treasure chest, and flips open the lid.

An odd smell strikes his nostrils and he scrunches his nose up. He runs his paw over the keys. "Eww," he says when he notices the keys feel a little sticky.

"Yeah, you'll need these," Gina says dropping a pack of disinfectant wipes onto the desk.

"Thank you," he smiles and turns around, but she's already walking away. He gives his new keyboard and monitors a vigorous wipe before plugging everything in. He lifts the monitor at the weird angle back to level. It slides down and he carefully pushes it back into place.

When he's done, he sits back, wipes his paws with three wipes and rubs them together excitedly.

"Here we go Colin," he says sticking out his chest. "You've hit the big time."

He leans forward and punches the power button

with a flourish. There's a whirr, a beep; and minute of silence.

Colin looks at the computer and raises his paw to press the Power button again, when suddenly the screen flashes, and the company wallpaper pops up on the left side computer monitor. The right one flashes twice, lets out an almost imperceptible crackle and goes dark before dropping back to its impossible angle. He looks at his functioning screen. It says it's nearly time for the annual - 'Hey. How you doin'?' - company engagement survey.

"Alright!" exclaims Colin and does another tiny paw-pump, a smile from ear to ear. "My own computer," he rubs his hands across the desk, "on my own desk, with my own nameplate." he squints at the post-it note and moves on. "In my first proper job." He waves to Brenda and George coming down the corridor. George waves back, but Brenda is to be too busy telling George how much work she has to do to notice.

"Now I have my computer, I can finally get to work and hopefully be as productive as Brenda," Colin says wistfully.

He turns back and squinches around in his chair in another unsuccessful attempt to get comfortable. He looks at the monitor and sees two empty login fields. Username and Password.

Colin sits back and looks around the desk to see if Randall been and left a note for him.

Nothing.

He double-checks his Special Reminder Notebook (even though he's 100% sure there was no information about login details) and can't find anything.

He looks over at Gina's desk, but it's empty again.

He scratches his chin, and slowly types: 'Colin', into the Username field, and moves to the Password. "Hmm," he scratches his head and tries to remember everything he knows about passwords.

His eyes light up and he quickly types the name of his first pet: 'Gordon', and presses Enter.

The screen says: 'Incorrect Login Details'.

He thinks again, and types the name of the street he grew up on: Eucalyptus Grove.

The screen says: 'Incorrect Login Details' again.

He scratches his chin and thinks hard. "AH!" he says and types in his mother's maiden name: 'Mum'.

A message pops up to say he one more attempt available, or he will be locked out of his account for 60 minutes.

"I'm already locked out of the account," Colin says quietly to himself, and unplugs the monitor so no-one else can see.

He folds his arms and taps his chin thoughtfully, when he notices a tall thin man out of the corner of his eye, walking towards him. He is wearing a neat shirt and a vest. 'He looks very organised', Colin thinks.

He peers closer to see if the man looks like a 'Randall' but can't tell.

Colin waves and calls out. "Hi. I'm Colin. I'm new here, and I don't know anything about how the company works. Could you please help me with something?"

The man smiles and introduces himself as Alfred, emphasising, "Alfred. Never Al," and says he will be happy to help. Colin explains about his new computer and asks if Alfred knows where he can find his Username and Password?

"Oh no, no," Alfred says shaking his head strongly. "I can't tell you my password. Alfred leans close and whispers. "It's very important to stay cybersafe, you should *never* ask anyone for their password."

Colin quickly tries to explain that he wasn't asking for *Alfred's* password. Only whether he knows where Colin could get *his* own password.

"I don't know your password," Alfred asserts, standing back up. "It's important to not share your password." He leans down again and glances around furtively. Colin glances as well, wondering what Alfred is looking for, but can't tell.

When Alfred stops looking, he whispers, "You should *never* tell anyone your password."

Colin opens his mouth to say he wasn't going to tell him his password, but Alfred jumps up and cries, "No!" throwing up his hands. "I don't want to know your password."

Colin tries again to explain that even if he wanted to tell Alfred, which he doesn't, that he couldn't, because he doesn't know what his password is. "Have you seen Randall? I think maybe Randall has it—" he starts.

Alfred holds up his hand to stop him again. "I hope not. No-one should know your password. It's a secret."

Colin explains that Randall is his Buddy and has the

information about his job, and is going to show him around, so it could make sense he might have his login details as well.

"Hmm," Alfred squints. "Whoever this Randall fellow is, if he knows your password, that makes him dangerous." He glances around furtively. "Very dangerous. You know you'll be responsible for anything he does using your login details," he shakes his head again. "If you think he knows your password, you should change it immediately," he nods definitively.

"Um. Okay, sure. Thanks," Colin smiles.

"My pleasure," Alfred replies. "Always best to stay safe," he gives Colin a casual salute and continues along the corridor.

Colin's shoulders slump as he watches Alfred walk off. "I just want to start my work," he says to his computer. He feels himself sliding involuntarily forward on his chair again, and resigns himself to sliding all the way off. "Maybe Gina knows my login details," he says to himself.

"No idea," she says without looking up. "You'll need to call the I.T. Support Help Desk. Number's in your employee handbook," she says, and wishes him luck.

"I think Randall is supposed to give me my employee handbook," Colin frowns and checks his watch. It's getting quite late, and he worries that he missed Randall when he was out getting coffee.

"...7, 4," Gina finishes.

"I'm sorry?" Colin says.

"The number for the I.T. Help Desk," Gina reads it out again.

"I.T. Help Desk," Colin nods. "That sounds like a crack team of highly skilled computer experts just waiting to provide quick and definitive assistance," he says as he copies the number down in his Special Reminder Notebook in case he ever needs it again.

"Yeah," Gina snorts. "That's them. An elite team of technical experts, who specialise in rapidly resolving important computer issues."

"Thanks!" Colin heads back to his desk. "I'll give them a call while I'm waiting for Randall."

"Sure," Gina says watching Colin skip back to his desk with a misplaced new-found sense of hope. "Who the hell is Randall?" she says to herself and shrugs.

Colin looks around carefully for anyone that might look like a Randall, and decides if he wants to get to work, it's best to contact the Support Desk.

He sits as comfortably as he can on the chair and slides forward again, as he dials the number. He hopes they won't be annoyed with him for calling with such a silly problem.

When the phone answers, a voice tells him that he should listen carefully, because the menu options have changed. Even though Colin doesn't know what the options were before, he listens extra carefully to the two options, wonders why they would change them, and selects option number one – 'I have a problem with my computer.'

After being presented with a new menu comprising of three new options that just seem to be – 'I have a problem with my computer' – said in three different ways, he selects option two – 'My computer is having problems'.

After two more menus of various re-wordings of - 'I have a problem with my computer', the phone is finally answered by a person.

"Thank you for calling the Help Desk, my name is Harry. I'm here to fix your problem."

Colin sits back in his chair impressed! Harry must be some kind of a super-expert to be so confident he can fix his problem before Colin has even told him what's wrong. Colin decides to call him 'Helpful Harry' and explains he needs his details to access his computer.

"Yes. I can definitely help you with that," Harry says confidently, and asks Colin if he is already logged in.

Colin checks that the phone is connected properly and repeats that the problem is that he isn't able to log in to his computer.

"Ah. It sounds like your computer is having a problem starting up and logging in," Helpful Harry confirms, and asks Colin if he has tried turning his computer off and on again to see if that fixes the problem.

Colin scratches his head and says he doesn't really

see how that would make a difference. But Harry assures him that many computer problems can be resolved by restarting.

"You're the expert," Colin says, knowing he isn't the one who's part of an elite team of technical experts who specialise in resolving computer issues the way Harry is, and restarts the computer.

After a few moments, Colin says he is back at the login screen.

"Excellent. Is there anything else I can help you with today?" Harry asks.

"Uh... Not yet," Colin says, and adds that he'd prefer to fix the problem with his login details first, before moving on to anything else.

Harry says, "Certainly. It sounds like you're having trouble logging into your computer. I can help you with that."

"Yes!" Colin smiles. "Now we're getting somewhere."

Harry says, "Often login problems are caused by an out-of-date password. You can reset your password. That will fix your problem."

Colin feels his jaw drop and he stares blankly at the

screen. "Um. But I... don't know my password."

"That's okay," says Harry cheerfully. "If you've forgotten your password, you can simply go to the 'Forgotten Password' link on the Intranet and reset it there."

Colin rubs his eyes and pushes on them hard enough that he can see kaleidoscopes and patterns. He takes a deep breath and holds it for a few seconds before explaining again slowly to Harry that today is his first day and he doesn't have his login details to get to the Intranet to reset his password. But quickly promises that he will reset it later, after he is able to login.

Harry says, "Ah. I understand. You're new and don't have your login details. Your Buddy may have them. Have you asked your Buddy?"

Colin says he hasn't met his Buddy yet, but would like to get started on his work as soon as possible because he's keen to 'add value'.

"Yes, of course," Harry says. "I understand. I can definitely help you with that," and places him on hold.

Colin listens to the hold music, which sounds like a jazz trumpet being played by someone who's never been exposed to music, and jumps expectantly when it stops, but then a recorded voice tells him: "Your call is important to us."

After a few more minutes of 'music', Harry comes back on.

"Good news," he says. "I can confirm your login details were emailed to you last week," he pauses. "But to be helpful, I have sent them to you again."

Colin says thank you, and asks Harry how he can get to get to his email to get his login details...

Helpful Harry says that because Colin is new, he will help him by talking him through how to open his email program.

POP! Goes the fur on top of Colin's head.

Colin tries unsuccessfully to press it back down, and rubs the back of his neck, which he notices is very tense. He begins to wonder if maybe he hadn't listened carefully *enough* to the menu options and had made the wrong selection.

Harry tells Colin to turn the computer on and to tell him when he sees a screen that has a field for his Username and Password.

Colin takes a deep breath and says he can see that

already.

"Enter your Username and Password and tell me when you can see the Start Menu," Harry says.

Colin reminds Harry that the reason he is calling is because he doesn't know his Username and Password.

Helpful Harry sighs and reminds Colin, "Your login details have been emailed to you," then adds with a sharp intake of breath, "twice."

For some reason Colin remembers the day at the carnival when the controller on the Merry-Go-Round had broken...

And it just kept spinning around, and around, and around, and no-one could stop it, and he had been sick all over his brand-new mid-range jacket and had needed to lie down for a long time.

"Coffee?" Graham appears beside him.

Colin says he would like that very much, but he is on the call to the Help Desk.

Graham smiles on one side of his mouth. "Right. And how's that working out for you?"

Colin says he was hoping to be put through to the special elite computer team Gina had mentioned, but he's not sure he dialled the right number.

After Graham stops laughing, he asks what the problem is. And laughs again when Colin tells him.

"You should have asked me," he says. "It's set up as a default," he points to the keyboard. "Just type in your first name and the initial of your last name. The password is Welcome123," Graham leans forward and whispers. "They say you're supposed to change it," he waves dismissively, "but nothing happens if you don't," he stands up and heads toward the lift. "I never have."

Colin types everything in, holds his breath, presses Enter and crosses his claws. For a moment nothing happens, then the login screen disappears, and he sees his desktop.

"YAY!" he yells and waves his paws in the air. "Why does my desktop already have lots of documents on it?"

Harry says he was glad he could help and that he will send Colin a survey after he hangs up, and asks Colin to give him a ten out of ten.

Colin jumps, because he had forgotten that he was still on the phone.

As he's hanging up, Bob the Boss appears. "Hey!" he beams. "Looks like Randall's got you all settled in," he points to the screen. "How are you going with your compulsory training? Finished?"

Colin gulps and explains he has only just managed to access his computer, but assures Bob he will get right onto it.

"Don't leave it too long," Bob says and turns back to the corridor. "Any questions, remember, just ask Randall," he says and disappears around the corner again.

He hears a 'Bing!' and see the notifications for the two emails that contain his login information pop-up, followed by an email asking him to complete a survey about how helpful Harry was, then a final reminder to complete the annual 'How you doin'?' company survey. He leans close and watches expectantly to see if there's an email from Randall, but nothing else arrives.

He sighs and spins around in his chair. Gina is staring intently at her phone. He can't see that she is reading her personal emails. Brenda is busy telling Alfred about her workload, who seems to be only half listening while he continues typing.

'Is this what a proper job is?' Colin thinks to himself, staring at the documents that belonged to whoever had the computer before, covering most of the desktop. There's several that contain the word 'Budget', others 'Confidential'. There's a folder titled: 'Personal - Do Not Delete' and a half the screen full of documents that are just number one to twenty-four.

The right hand monitor screen flashes on and off once.

Colin sighs. He'd been expecting a shiny, brand-new computer, not one that takes ages to start, has sticky keys and fourteen folders with different variations of the name 'Bullshit' on the desktop.

"I'm in," he calls to Gina who still has her headphones in and just waves back.

He opens a new email and types 'Randall' into the TO field. Only one name appears, so he sends and email to ask if he is his Buddy and where can he find him.

"Maybe they don't think I'm worth it," he says softly, looks at his nameplate with the post-it note that makes it read 'Colli N', and wriggles back up in the uncomfortable chair. He slumps forward and rests his cheeks in his paws on the desk.

Bing! Goes his computer again. The email is an

auto-reply from Randall from a year earlier saying he has left the company.

Bing! goes his email program. Colin looks over with one eye and sees an email from Bob.

It says, "Glad to have you on board Collie. Now that Randall has you squared away, I'd like you to get started on this spreadsheet. The person who looked after it before didn't have a lot of experience with them, so I think it's not set up the most efficient way. If you could clean it up and make it easier to use, then plug last month's data into it, that'd be great. It needs to be ready to go into the monthly report tomorrow. Thanks, Bob."

Bing! goes the computer again and he checks the email. It reads: "Your Security Pass is ready for collection."

Bing! It goes again with an email from Graham saying he has volunteered to be Colin's Buddy in Randall's place.

As Colin is typing a response to Graham, another email arrives from George, welcoming him on board and providing a list of social activities.

Colin flicks back to Bob's email and opens the

spreadsheet. He jumps back in the chair.

"Not efficient!" he rubs his eyes and stares at it. "I've seen magpie nests more organised than this," he mumbles and scrolls down. The more he sees, the worse it gets. "It looks like it was created by that trumpet player on the phone."

He checks his watch. Nearly three o'clock. He looks around the office. Brenda is still loudly talking to someone across the hall, everyone rushing past her in a hurry.

Colin pushes himself back up into the chair and stares at the train wreck of a spreadsheet in front of him.

He takes a deep breath, pauses, and finally says, "YES!"

He fist-pumps the air with his paw and bounces up and down. "Lets' get this show on the road!" he cracks his knuckles and pulls the mouse and keyboard towards him. "Your first assignment, Colin the Koala, at your very own desk, on your own computer, in your first real job; is to tame this spreadsheet for your Boss."

He glances around the office again and can't stop

the huge smile that's spreading across his face. "You've made it Colin," he says, and puffs out his chest. "You've really made it."

He turns back to the screen and sets his mouth purposefully. "Alright Mr. Spreadsheet. It's time you got yourself under control."

He opens a blank document.

"And *I'm* just the Koala to do it."

There's No I in T E A M

"I don't think we've got time for coffee," Colin says checking his watch as he struts down the corridor with Graham. "Our team building session starts in ten minutes and I'm excited to get to work on becoming a high-performing team," he smiles broadly and high fives a surprised co-worker coming the other way.

"First of all," Graham steps sideways to avoid the person's attempt to high five him as well and points at Colin with his re-usable coffee cup that reads - 'This meeting should have been an email'. "There's always time for coffee. Second of all, this team crap is pointless. Just the latest management flavour of the month."

"Well, *I'm* excited," Colin bounces up and down as they wait for the lift. "Bob the Boss said he has hired a crack squad of team building professionals who can align us to our common goals and focus us on achieving together, moulding a rag-tag group of individuals into..." his voice raises in volume as he concludes dramatically, "a High-Performing Team!" He checks his watch again and does a quick mental calculation. "I'm going to go to the room," he says and waves goodbye as Graham steps into the lift. "I don't want to miss anything."

"Yeah. That's just it though," Graham starts as the doors close. "We just got allocated under Bob because they didn't have anywhere else to put us. We don't have any common purpo—"

Colin strides along the corridor and into the meeting room. As he finds a seat, he thinks about all the times he had wanted to be part of a high-performing team. Like the time he had volunteered to be the anchor runner on the 200 metre sprint relay team, but had been passed over because they said his legs were too short. When he had tried out to be centre on the basketball team, the opposing team hadn't even noticed he was there, because no-one had looked down.

As he sits down and waves hello to Alfred, he remembers his brief period in Ms Seal's Synchronised Swimming Squad. At the time he thought it sounded very exciting, but after what is now known as - 'The Noseplug Incident', he had admitted to himself that he had been more enticed by the alliteration than the activity.

"Alright. Let's get started," Bob the Boss claps his hands for attention. "

"Where's Gina?" Umi asks looking around the room.

"I needed her to do some work for me, so she won't be able to come along," Bob says and motions for the two team building professionals to come forward and start the session.

"But isn't she part of the team?" Umi frowns. "How will we become a team is she isn't here?"

"I have work to do as well," Brenda pushes herself up from the designer chair that's too low to easily get up from, until she sees Bob glaring at her. "I don't see why she gets out of this…"

"Let's move on," Bob interrupts and introduces the Team Building professionals; Michael and Micaela. He reads off the note they had given him before the session outlining their background in successful team development, and some of the other businesses they have worked with.

Michael and Micaela step forward energetically and introduce themselves by repeating the information that Bob has just provided. Michael is holding a box draped with purple velvet.

'I wonder if that's a magical box,' Colin thinks, looking forward to becoming a high-performing team member. 'It looks magical.'

"Yes George?" Bob points to George's raised hand.

'Good asking George,' nods Colin. He knows that it is important to put up your hand and wait your turn, not to just interrupt, the way Bob sometimes does.

"If we all promise to work together as a team," George looks around, "can we skip this rubbish and go to the pub?"

Colin watches Michael pretend to laugh for a moment and then suddenly pull a card from the magical box he's holding. "No, we're going to do something much, much better," he says.

"And much more fun?" claps Micaela, her voice rising up at the end of the statement, making it sound like a question.

"George, you know it's only ten o'clock, right?" Bob chimes in.

Michael carefully studies the card he has produced. "Okay," he stops and squints purposefully at everyone in the room. "I want you to pretend you're a type of bread," he pauses dramatically. "What type of bread would you be?"

"Dinner roll!" Colin yells, and wraps his arms over his head to look like a roll. "Because it's small, but packed full of excitement," he giggles.

"I've got work I need to do," Brenda stands up but Bob waves at her to sit back down.

Umi taps her chin, "I think I'd be sourdough.," she nods.

"I'm think I'm unsliced bread," Alfred calls out.

"I don't think that's what she means," Bob glares over at him.

"All good choices?" says Micaela her voice rising at the end of the sentence again as she smiles. "And what about you?" she says pointing to Vanessa.

Vanessa stares back at her, arms folded and expressionless.

Colin leans forward and leans on his paws, 'Gosh. Look at her concentration,' he thinks.

Micaela's eyes flick quickly back and forth from Vanessa, to Michael and Bob, then back to Vanessa. She coughs once and shifts her feet from side to side.

After a few more moments, she decides that Vanessa mustn't have realised she was talking to her and repeats slowly, pointing directly at Vanessa, "Pretend you are a type of bread—"

"I'm unable to respond," Vanessa says flatly. "Bread isn't sentient. It's inanimate."

Colin falls back in his chair and slaps his forehead. "Gosh! She's right," he says to himself, second guessing whether he jumped in with his answer too soon. He knows that for the team to be high-performing, needs to be at the top of his game as well.

"I'd be white bread..." calls Bill before Micaela can respond to Vanessa.

"Of course you would," Brenda snorts from the back. "I've got things to do—"

"Although I can't actually have bread, you know," Bill continues as though there'd been no gap from his previous sentence. "I'm gluten intolerant."

Bob stands up and takes a deep breath. "I don't think that matters for the purpose of this exercise Bill."

Bill moves himself straight in the chair and glares directly at Bob, "Oh, I think you'll find it does," he says emphatically, "if I have even a whiff of gluten, my digestive system goes into overload. My wife says she can hear the grumbling from the next room—"

"Are you sure she's talking about your stomach?"

Bob holds his hand up, "Okay. We don't need to know Bill, thank you."

Bill ignores them both, "And when I get to the toilet, oh my god—"

"Stop!" everyone yells together.

"What did I miss?" Graham asks, walking into the room.

"Don't ask."

"The session started ten minutes ago," Bob points emphatically at his watch.

"Alright..." Micaela says slowly, "I think that's everyone? Good answers?" she declares, her voice rising at the end again.

"Why is she asking if you had good answers?" Graham whispers to Colin.

"Great work team," Michael claps encouragingly, reaching in to pull out another card from the magic box. "Oooh," he says, "this is a good one. If you had the choice between flying or having x-ray vision. Which would you choo—"

"X-ray vision," Graham responds quickly, pulling a chair off to one side.

"Wow," Michael jumps back, eyes wide in surprise. "I've never had someone answer that quickly."

Colin leans forward and points at Graham. "High performer," he nods.

"I'm intrigued by your decisiveness," Michael takes a step toward Graham. "Why would you choose x-ray vision?"

Graham looks at him blankly. "I can go to the airport and buy a ticket to fly," Graham glances round the room, "I can't buy x-ray vision."

From the corner of his eye, Colin notices Bob's head fall forward.

"Uh... That's not quite the way this game goes..."

Michael looks at Graham. Graham's expression reminds him of the expression of his four year old nephew who'd insisted Michael had to actually swallow the play-doh food on his plate for the game to work, and makes a mental note to spend the weekend re-assessing his choice of career.

Again.

"It's not like he's going to regret his decision," Alfred jumps in. "He's not actually going to gain x-ray vision and wish he had chosen flight."

Michael's eyes flick over to Bob for guidance. Bob makes a show of looking at his watch, then spins his index finger in tight circles, signalling to speed things up.

"Maybe it's break time," Micaela leaps in, "Can we say fifteen minutes?"

"Okay everyone. Let's take a 15 minute break," Bob jumps up quickly in front of Micaela, calculating how long it will take him to get to the donut shop and back. "Fifteen minutes only," he wags his finger sternly, deciding that if he rushes, he could make it there and back in just under twenty, and turns to Michael. "I've got a few important emails I need to respond to. I'll do what I can, but I'm guessing I'll need at least half an hour or so. Start without me."

"Who wants coffee?" Graham jumps up from his chair. "I'll get the money from petty cash afterwards," he calls to Bob who is already out the door.

Colin is impressed by how considerate Graham is to make sure everyone has a cup of coffee, even though Graham has only just finished the one he had, and they all quickly agree that coffee is a great idea.

Colin jumps up, "I'm a Team Player!" he declares, and says he is happy to help. He makes sure to write all the coffee orders in his Special Reminder Notebook, so he doesn't forget.

"Alright everyone," Michael taps his empty wrist. "Fifteen minutes. Synchronise watches."

"I can never understand why in movies, they say, 'synchronise watches' and then all nod," George says as Colin writes down their coffee orders, "but no-one ever asks anyone else, 'what time do you have?'"

Colin grasps his Special Reminder Notebook tightly as

he and Graham join the queue at the coffee shop.

"Looks like someone's in a hurry," Graham nudges Colin and points towards a man in a backwards baseball cap bouncing from side to side looking over everyone's shoulders towards the counter before checking his watch and looking over at the counter again.

"He must have somewhere very important to be," Colin nods back. "Maybe he's a key member of a high-performing team."

"Yeah... maybe..." Graham says unconvincingly, watching the cap bounce from side to side in front of him.

When the man eventually gets to the counter, he huffs. "About time," then looks up at the menu to decide what he wants to order.

".... or maybe he's not."

"What a silly-billy," Colin shakes his head. "He could have used all that time he was waiting to decide what to order."

Graham folds his arms and nods, "Yeah, but I don't think 'silly-billy' is the word you're looking for. I think the word you're looking for is cun—"

"Next!"

Graham plonks his re-usable coffee cup that reads, 'If I agreed with you, we'd both be wrong' onto the counter.

Colin looks over the counter at the barista's shirt. "Hi Barry," he smiles, reading the name sown onto the flannel shirt. "We're buying lots of coffees for our soon to be high-performing team," he declares proudly. "You can copy them from here," he opens up his Special Reminder Notebook and holds the page where he had written down the coffee orders high so Barry the barista can see it over the counter.

The barista, who considers himself far too cool to inform Colin that he found the shirt in an op-shop and has no idea who Barry is, instead twirls his moustache between his tattooed fingers. "Just tell me. I'll be fine," he says and makes noises with his steam machine.

"Okay…" Colin takes a deep breath and reads them out for him. "A strong oat milk latte with six sweeteners for Vanessa. Two cappuccinos - one with Almond milk and caramel syrup for Umi, the other with lite milk and four sugars for George. A piccolo for Bob the Boss. One long black, but not too long," he points to Graham, "for my friend Graham," he smiles, "a cappuccino with extra chocolate for me," and checks the final entry, "and something called a Mocha for Bill."

"A *mocha* for Bill?" Graham looks over quizzically.

Colin shrugs. "He said he didn't feel like having a coffee."

Graham looks over at Barry, who makes it clear he is ignoring the conversation, then back to Colin. "What do you mean he doesn't want a 'coffee'?" Graham squints.

"Dunno," Colin says. "But Bill told me that 'Mocha' means 'mock-coffee'."

"Uh..." Graham blinks twice, "I don't think it does..."

Colin shrugs, "Bill told me that every Saturday morning he takes his Grandkids to the park, and afterwards he buys them each a large mock-coffee before he drops them back home."

Graham raises an eyebrow at the barista whose name isn't Barry.

"Bill says they love spending time with him," Colin continues. "He says they're so thrilled with his visits they can barely contain themselves. They run around and around in excitement."

"What's the name for the coffees?" the barista whose name isn't Barry asks, pen in hand.

"Colin," Colin says slowly holding up his Special Reminder Notebook with the coffee orders again. "Are you sure you don't want to..."

"I'm good," Not Barry says, turning away smugly.

After a few minutes, Colin checks his watch. "I'm worried we're going to be late back," he frowns.

"You know it doesn't matter," Graham replies stepping back to avoid the backward baseball cap man, who is pacing and tutting impatiently. When his coffee arrives he takes a sip and stares at the cup, "I don't know if this is what I want now."

"Definitely a cun—"

"Coffees for Kelvin." The barista whose name isn't Barry calls, pushing two trays across the counter.

"Colin?" Colin asks, lifting his eyebrows hopefully.

Not Barry lifts the tray and checks the name. "Says Kelvin. Nine coffees."

Colin sighs and wants to say, "Even if you wrote my name down wrong, I ordered them less than five minutes ago," but knows that would be impolite, so instead he reaches up to the counter. "Thank you. They'll be for me..."

"That's a very interesting question," George rubs his chin carefully. "You know, I've never really thought about it," he stares up at the ceiling, as Michael holds the marker to write the answer on the whiteboard. "I think if I had the choice to have a meal with anyone, alive or dead..." he nods at Michael, "I'd choose lunch."

"Uh..." Michael's hand drops to his side and glances over his shoulder looking for Bob, who's not back yet, for support.

"I think lunch would be best," George turns confidently to Vanessa. "That way, if it's going well, you can extend it out into the afternoon. If it's not, you can say you have to get back to work and cut it short."

Vanessa nods in agreement. "Good point."

Michael turns blankly to Micaela who shrugs, pauses, decides that it might be time to move on and suddenly yells, "Shoe game!" causing Michael to jump and drop the blue marker, which lands, tip down, onto his shoe before bouncing onto the floor.

"I'm really enjoying the team building session," Colin smiles carefully skipping over a hole in the footpath. "I'm worried we're missing something important though. The coffees took longer than I expected."

"Ha! Yeah, I remember when I was young and keen like you and would lap this stuff up," Graham laughs.

Colin stares up at Graham as though he had just declared himself to be a purple cow.

Graham looks back and thinks for a second, "Yeah, you're right. That doesn't sound like me," he says narrowly avoiding a man in a suit whizzing past on a motorised skateboard.

"I see us moving forward to greatness," Colin waves his arm forward majestically, balancing the coffee tray on one paw. "Working together like a well-oiled machine, leveraging synergies to create a high-functioning cohort that's greater than the sum of its parts."

"Are you okay?" Graham looks down at Colin, concerned. "Do I need to call an Ambulance?"

Colin ignores him and pushes the crossing button. "I'm serious. It's been well documented that people with a common goal work more efficiently, have higher morale, and are more productive and innovative working together as part of a team."

"I'm not sure how identifying what type of bread I am is going to make me more efficient," Graham replies as the light changes to green and they step onto the road.

Colin jumps out of the way of a man with a pram, rushing to get past.

"People with prams are pushy," Graham watches the man disappear along the street.

"I'm sure the bread thing is just an introduction," Colin says; hopefully. If he was being honest, he wasn't sure how it would help them be more aligned to a common goal, unless they all quit tomorrow to work in a bakery. "We should hurry, I'm sure we're missing an important productivity-improving exercise that will help us think so differently about the way we manage our work it will blow our minds."

"Okay. Everyone quickly form a neat circle?" Micaela yells, her voice rising. "This game is great for improving productivity, managing time and changing the way you think about the way you manage your work?"

"Sorry I'm late," Bob stage whispers as he slips in through the door. "Important business," he over-emphasises an apologetic shrug causing several pieces of donut glaze to drop from his collar onto the floor. He quickly brushes them away with his foot. "But this exercise sounds like it's exactly what we need."

"And it's fun too!" chimes in Michael as he motions everyone to gather into a circle, and breathlessly explains the rules. "In this game, everyone takes off their shoes and puts them over by this wall."

Michael pulls off his shoes to demonstrate and frowns at the blue spot near the lace as he places them against the wall. "Then we all stand over here," he says, jogging to the opposite wall.

"Is he okay?" Gina mouths to Bob as he sits back down next to her.

"Then I'll say a fact about a someone in the team," he says, "and you run across the room as fast as you can," he calls and mimes running across the room to the shoes—"

"What?" Pooja looks around at the confused faces.

"The first one to grab the shoes of the person that the fact is about; is the winner?" Micaela makes a series of tiny claps as she bounces up and down on her toes.

"Is that a question?"

"And the winner gets to read the next fact on the list," Michael lifts the list and his shoes, and bounces energetically as though he just won gold at the Olympics.

"I don't understand what you're saying."

"I'm not touching anyone's shoes."

"I don't know what's happening."

"Why do you keep yelling?"

"Okay everyone," yells Micaela, "Shoes off?" she slips her runners off and places them neatly against the wall as Michael returns his.

"Can you repeat the instructions again please?" Bill asks scratching his head. "I really don't understand what we're doing here."

Michael's hands drop slowly down to his sides as he slumps.

As Michael is about to explain the game - 'who's shoe in the zoo' again, the door slides open and Graham and Colin appear with the coffees.

"Oh, thank you sweet Jesus," Bob looks up to heaven and leaps from his chair, which tilts precariously on its back legs for a moment. He grabs the tray from Colin as the chair rights itself with a clunk.

Colin climbs up on his seat to tell everyone how clever the coffee man was to remember all their orders, while Bob confidently hands out the coffees, making out that he was somehow responsible for getting them.

"Why does it smell like feet in here?" Graham sniffs as he puts the other tray on the table.

"Who had the flat white?" Bob asks, holding out one of the cups.

"Is this almond milk?"

"Who's Kelvin?"

"Uh oh." Colin says and shakes his head. "It looks like Barry's memory isn't as good as he thinks it is," he laughs and holds up his Special Reminder Notebook. "That's why I carry this." It reminds him of the time at Maisy the Magpie's birthday party. The Kangaroo brothers had gotten into an argument because Scott had brought his brother the wrong type of beer. Colin doesn't want the team building session to turn into another impromptu boxing match.

"Who had the chai tea?"

"None of these are right."

After a brief conference to clarify that no, there wasn't enough time for another coffee excursion to get the order right, Bob declares they should carry on. "It's a shame the order is wrong, but there's no need to hold Graham responsible."

"What? Who's holding me responsible?"

"Let's not focus on that," Bob says quickly. "We'll just make the best of what we have. Like working together as a team." Bob leans back in his chair and nods sagely. Impressed by his ability to link the situation back to the task at hand.

Colin takes a sip of his coffee and splutters twice. "Ugh. What is this?" he examines the cup for any kind of clue. "I want to get away from my tongue..."

"Ahem," Micaela interrupts.

"Oh sorry," Colin apologises and carefully places the cup down as though it might explode. "Go on." He grabs a gum leaf from his pencil case to try and remove the taste.

Michael watches him pop the leaf into his mouth, "Uh, should you be going to a smoking area or something with that?"

Colin stops chewing and turns to Bob. He'd never considered that before.

"I'm not sure it's covered in Policy," Bob declares. "Let's move it along."

"Great," Michael smiles. "Let's get back to Team Building business," he checks his watch and frowns. "We're a little behind, and we've still got a bit to get through."

Colin leans forward and readies himself. "I'm ready to become a high-performing team member," he says proudly and cocks one ear to listen carefully.

He finds a new blank page in his Special Reminder Notebook and takes notes as Michael and Micaela take turns explaining the benefits of working as a high-performing team.

Michael writes across the top of the whiteboard - Teams work together to achieve greatness, by focusing on the importance of their common purpose and aligned goals.

He stops and looks around the room like he's waiting for a round of applause. When none eventuates, he draws a series of columns and begins to question each person about their individual goals and tasks.

Colin sits up straight and takes notes about the way Michael asks probing, open ended questions to gain answers and insight into everyone's tasks and functions. He's especially impressed by the way Michael switches marker colours to create links between items that initially seemed disconnected.

"May I ask a clarifying question?" Vanessa asks raising her hand.

Colin smiles at Vanessa's politeness, and make a note to tell her later how impressed he is.

"Of course," Michael smiles.

Vanessa looks around the room and says, "We don't have common goals or purpose."

Michael opens his mouth. "Uh..." he waits awkwardly for a few moments, "and, uh, your question..."

"Hmm." Vanessa frowns and shrugs. "I guess I don't have a question. Maybe it's more of a clarifying statement."

Michael assures them that they don't need to worry, because every team has common goals and purpose, and he's sure they just haven't considered them yet. "That's why we're here today," he say confidently.

Micaela picks up a marker and a sketches a series of arrows and interlocking lines across the board. She steps back and assesses her additions and taps her chin thoughtfully, leaving a series of tiny green dots, Colin watches as she leaps forward again to attack the board the way his friend Whiskers the Crow would peck at the bits of food stuck to the tar on the side of the burning highways.

After one final pause, Micaela makes a circle across the middle with a flourish, and wipes her forehead with the back of her hand.

"We'll just grab a drink of water and let you ingest this," she says and waves Michael to follow her out of the room.

Colin looks between the board and his notes in an attempt to understand what he should be 'ingesting'.

The rest of the team stare at the board as the clock on the back wall tick-tocks the seconds away.

"Looks like a Pro Hart painting," Bill suddenly laughs.

"No-one knows who that is."

"Well," Bill folds his arms and leans back, "Pro Hart is a well-known Australian abstract painter, who—"

"It doesn't matter who he is," Vanessa interrupts.

Bob jumps up to save the day. "I think it proves what we all knew deep down," he says pointing at the colourful mess on the board.

"That this a waste of time?"

"No!"

Brenda stands up and declares, "Are we finished? This is taking up too much of my time. I've already got so much work to do you wouldn't believe it..."

"I think it's all bulls—"

"Okay, there's need for that," calls Bob.

Colin looks around at the rest of the team muttering and complaining. Michael and Micaela have worked hard to help them all be more efficient and improve their morale. And feels his jaw beginning to clench. Why can't they all work together?

"All I want to do," Colin calls out to help them get back onto the ingesting, but no-one hears him over the chatter. He feels the muscles in his neck begin to tense. "All I want to do," he repeats louder, still with no success in getting over the cross-talk.

He takes a deep breath and says with his loudest and deepest voice, "All I want to do," he drops down from his chair as the room begins to go quiet. "Is make our company successful, help us all enjoy our time at work more, and be productive," he stands tall in the middle of the room addressing the team. "Michael and Micaela just worked their arses - excuse my French - off, and have shown us everything we need to know to do exactly that," he stares at each one of them, breathing quickly. "It's..." he opens his Special Reminder Notebook, "vital for a high-performing team to understand and align to a common goal and purpose, and we can't even agree on—"

"I think we've all agreed this is a waste of time, haven't we?" Brenda surveys the room for support, but finds none.

Colin slams the book shut and stares at them, his heart beating like a hummingbird inside his tiny chest. "I don't want to come to work every day and just trudge through the day working on my own, doing the bare minimum."

Gina opens her mouth then decides now might not be the right time to make a 'bear' joke.

"I want to come to work," Colin paces across the room, "and be part of a team. To work together with all of you to help each of us become better at what we do. Be more focused and efficient," he paces back again. "And for us all to be happier. We spend five days a week together. We should want to have more fun and—"

"Everything okay?' Michael asks slowly moving back into the room.

Colin stops. "Oh," he says and looks around the room. "Oh. I'm sorry," he says softly and walks slowly back to his chair.

"There's no need to apologise for your commitment Colin," Bob jumps up and walks to the front. "Maybe if others could take a leaf from your..." he pauses uncomfortably, "well, not an actual leaf, a—"

"I know what you mean," Colin says, mistakenly sipping his coffee out of habit and grimacing.

"Thank you," Bob nods. "If others were as devoted as you, then maybe we *could* transform ourselves into a high-performing t—"

"Alright, alright. I agree with Colin," Graham suddenly jumps up. "He's just trying to help us make things better for ourselves." he says looking at Micaela and pointing to the board, "So," he waves his hand, "we need to align to a common goal and purpose... Go. What do we need to do?"

Michael and Micaela look at each other, then the team, then down at the ground. "We, um, can't find one," Michael mumbles.

"Can't find one what?" Bob scratches his head.

"As far as we can tell, the only thing that this team has in common is that they all report to you," Micaela points at Bob.

"Told you."

Colin drops back into his chair and slumps down. 'How will I ever be part of a high-performing team that increases efficiency and morale and helps the business become more productive without common goals and purpose?' he thinks noticing the tiny green dots on Micaela's chin and the blue spot on Michael's shoe. He glances at the still full cups of coffee marked 'Kelvin' that have gone cold on the table. He sighs and looks back at the board. "I'll never be part of a high-performing team."

"Of course you will?" Micaela claps suddenly, causing Michael to drop the marker onto his other shoe.

"You might not have a specific goal for your team, but you still have a common purpose to help make the business successful?" Micaela continues.

"Was that a question?"

"And to make the business successful," Michael says glancing at the matching marks on his shoes, but realising Micaela might be onto something. "You need to be able to support each other as a team to help each other be the best you can be."

"That's right Michael?" Micaela yells. "And that can be the most high-performing team of all?"

Colin feels his muscles tense and his jaw clench again, but this time in excitement. "I can be part of the most high-performing team of all!"

"A team is built on trust!" Michael claps. "What do you think team? Do we have trust in our team?"

"Why does he keep yelling?" George leans over to Vanessa, who shrugs back.

"Okay George, thanks for volunteering for our trust game," Michael says slowly, with a tiny hint of annoyance thrown in. "Who else would like to volunteer?"

Colin throws his hand up so quickly he nearly tips backwards off the chair.

"Okay! Yes. Colin," Michael points at him. "Can you both come up to the front please?" he waves his hand in a big wide arc tracing out the route from their seats to the front of the room, so they don't get lost on the way.

Colin is so excited he scurries to the front and gets there before George.

Micaela tells the team that this exercise is called a

'Trust Fall' and that it's important to teamwork because it helps everyone understand how we can trust each other to catch us when we need them.

"I don't really fall over that much," George says as he walks past Michael.

"Everyone needs to find a partner," Michael ignores him, "and pair up into groups of two."

After an awkward thirty seconds of stillness, everyone slowly pushes themselves, amid groans and mumbling, out of their chairs.

"Sorry," Graham puts his hand up, "how many people did you say we needed to have in our pair group?"

"Two," Michael says helpfully.

"So, we should have only two people in our pair group?" Vanessa looks around, checking how many people are in other's pair group. "Is that correct?"

"Yes. That's correct." Michael nods. "Now in a second what will happen is one person from the pair will stand in front of the other and fall backwards. The 'trust' part of the—. Yes, Graham?"

"Okay, so, just to make sure I'm on the same page. Our pair should only have two pe—"

"Yes," growls Bob. "Two," and glares at Graham.

"What?" Graham says holding his arms wide innocently, "I'm just trying to make sure I've got it right," and counts loudly to make sure there are two people in his pair group. "One. Two," he nods definitively. "We're good to go."

"As I was saying," says Michael, "the trust part of the exercise is that the front person trusts the back person to catch them—"

"There's nine of us," interrupts Gina.

Michael stops again, "Yes..."

"I don't have a partner to pair up with," she says, folding her arms, "into a group of two."

"Just join one of the other groups," Micaela says sharply, her voice suddenly flat.

Michael continues. "This exercise will help you build reliance and trus—. Sigh. Yes Graham?"

"We've got three people in our pair group of two now," he says pointing at himself, Vanessa and Gina.

"Just take turns!" Micaela slams her hand on the table.

Graham, Vanessa and Gina move into different configurations, "How do we know which order to..."

"Thanks to Colin and George for volunteering to demonstrate," Michael forges on ignoring them. "The idea... *again*... is that one person will fall backwards, and the other team member catches them."

Behind him Colin smiles at George and prepares himself.

"Are you sure this is a good idea?" says Pooja, rubbing the back of her neck and pointing over Michael's shoulder.

Michael looks around and sees Colin, one foot solidly in front of the other. Paws wide apart. Jaw set in concentration. "I'm ready George!" he yells.

"Oh shit!" Michael leaps and knocks Colin out of the way as George starts his fall backwards.

The next day, Bob calls a special meeting to discuss the Team Building session. Colin is excited to talk more about how successful the day was as they all file into the room. He waves excitedly at Michael and Micaela and notices that Bob has also invited Lacey from Legal, and Sally from Safety to join in too. Colin thinks that it's probably because the day was so successful, they must want to run one for their teams too.

When Graham comes in, carrying his re-usable coffee cup that simply reads, 'Nope', he waves, gives a hearty "Hi!" and is disappointed that Michael won't let him write on his cast.

They all spend the next half hour talking with Lacey from Legal. She is extremely interested in the trust exercise, but seems a little muddled by it, and asks four different people to repeat it. Colin is impressed at how smart she is, so he listens very carefully. She knows lots of words Colin hasn't heard before like, 'liability,' and 'negligence,' and 'lawsuit.'

They all listen carefully to Lacey's questions and talk through the day. Pooja helps Umi remember the shoe game rules. Graham remembers he needs to talk to Bill about 'mocha' and says they'll catch up after the meeting.

After everyone has had the chance to talk, Lacey says the meeting is over and everyone can go. Everyone except Bob. She says she needs to speak with him alone to discuss the stories that Michael and

Micaela had told her about the day; and what that might mean for his career.

"Looks like Bob's getting a promotion," Colin nudges Graham. "Well deserved. The day was a great success."

"Success?" Lacey stares at Colin. "How on earth was it a success?"

"You heard how we all helped each other in this meeting today. And you should have seen everyone working together yesterday: Graham called Aida the First Aider, while Umi, Pooja and Alfred helped George back to his chair. Gina rang for Sally from Safety, and Vanessa and Bill had made sure Michael remained comfortable; and conscious, until help arrived," he turned to Michael, noticing the bruise under his eye for the first time. "Michael and Micaela are definitely experts at Team Building," he turns back to Bob and folds his arms confidently.

"Congratulations on your career chat Boss," Colin smiles. "I hope they don't move you too high up and you'll come back to visit us sometime."

There's an opportunity to expand your role

Koala

Colin the Koala licks his paw and smooths down the small tuft of fur on the top of his head again.

"Sorry Boss," he says and shrugs apologetically. "I'm not sure why it keeps doing that. I really am finding my first one-on-one valuable."

Bob the Boss watches as the tuft of fur pops up again, and uncrosses his legs. "Tell me again why you're dressed like that?" he points at Colin's clothing.

Colin looks down at his basketball outfit and mumbles, "It's complicated." Pretending he's not disappointed that this meeting isn't what he had expected when he'd accepted the invitation.

Bob checks his watch. "We're almost out of time," he uncrosses his legs and realises his foot has gone to sleep. "Oh. That reminds me," Bob jumps back in the chair, pretending he had just remembered the item that was the real reason he originally called the meeting. "I'd like to give you the opportunity to expand your role," he smiles, "and take over for Brenda while she's on leave," he says, tapping his foot gingerly on the floor.

Brenda's job! Colin's tiny brow furrows. He knows that Brenda is constantly overloaded with work because she's always coming around telling everyone how busy she is!

Bob swings his foot around to try and wake it up. "It's a great chance to show how you can 'step-up'."

Colin sucks in a quick breath and hopes Bob isn't referring to the obscure '90s dance film series of the same name; he never could quite get the hang of the moves because of his short legs. He makes a note in his Special Reminder Notebook for when he gets home to check the downstairs cupboard for his VHS tapes just in case. "But wouldn't... Vanessa... be better?" Colin asks reluctantly. "Brenda is always talking to her about her work."

Bob re-crosses his legs, placing his numb foot on the top so he can rub it. "You're right," he says, moving his foot as the circulation begins to come back. "And I know Vanessa would jump at the chance if I asked her," he nods seriously (knowing that he would rather jump into a shark tank wearing a wetsuit made of offal than ask her). "But I think this could be an important rung on your career ladder," he points at Colin with the tip of his pen. " *Very* important," he smiles encouragingly, even though he knows from personal experience that care-taking someone else's role has absolutely zero influence on any future promotional decisions. "In fact, I think you should add it to your Career Development Plan. Performance Review time is coming up."

"That sounds exciting," Colin sits up straight. "What's a performance review?" he asks and adds quickly, "Do I get one?"

"Ha, ha. Of course you get one," Bob shakes his head and smiles. "Everyone gets one. It's a review of your performance over the past year to highlight how well you've performed and areas for growth. It includes your Career Development Plan."

Colin rubs his paws together. "It certainly does sound exciting."

Bob looks out through the glass wall at his team, "That's not what most people call it," then back to Colin. "Yes, it is," he lies. "*And* this will be an activity I will be able to highlight during the Bell-curving sessions."

"Bell...curving?" Colin reaches up and lightly touches his ear. He hopes the bells won't be too loud. It's hard for him to find earplugs in his size.

"Never mind that for now," Bob feels his stomach rumble and realises it's past his usual donut time. "This is a *great* opportunity," he says checking his watch. "And not one I give out lightly. Anyway, I've got another important meeting to get to."

Colin smiles, "It *does* sound like a great opportunity," he agrees helpfully, even though he has no real idea what Brenda does, or whether he has any interest in doing her job.

Bob wriggles his numb foot in a small circle to try and speed up the returning blood flow. "I've already let Brenda know that you'll be in touch with her to get a rundown of her main activities," Bob says tapping his foot again.

"Okay," Colin says climbing down from his chair. "Thank you for the opportunity. I won't hold you up any longer for your important meeting."

"I wanted to run it by you first," Bob stalls for time and winces slightly as the circulation begins to return to his foot. "It's important for a good leader to not simply spring work on their team members without consultation and their agreement first."

"Thanks Boss," Colin says walking towards the door, and decides it might be impolite to ask why Brenda is already expecting a call from him when this is the first time Colin is aware of it. "Uh. Didn't you need to..." he turns back when he realises Bob is still sitting.

"Yes," Bob taps his numb foot on the ground a few times. "But it's important to me that you're comfortable to step-up before I lock this in."

"Yes. I think so Boss," Colin thinks and takes a few steps back towards his chair. "I'm not as busy as Brenda, but I do have quite a lot to do."

"I know Colin, you deserve a pat on the back. You're doing a *great* job," Bob says leaning forward.

To Colin it looks as though he's emphasising the word *great*, but Bob is actually testing whether his foot can support his weight.

Colin puffs out his chest, "Aww. Thanks Boss," he says and reaches his paw over his shoulder to give himself a pat on the back.

Bob nods, impressed again by his ability to provide useful and timely feedback to his team. "Obviously, it *will* mean a bit more work for you," he slowly puts some more weight on his leg to confirm it's going to support him before committing to closing the meeting.

Colin makes a note in his Special Reminder Notebook:

Boss says I'm doing a 'great' job :)

"You'd better get to your important meeting Boss," Colin checks his watch. "Thank you for taking the extra time with me."

"That's the role of a good leader Colin," Bob pushes himself out of the chair and tentatively places his foot down to walks towards the door.

"I can't wait to learn more about Performance Reviews," Colin takes a moment to make a note in his Special Reminder Notebook to ask Bob about them next time before he closes it; and repeats Bob's comment quietly to himself, "You've been doing a *great* job Colin," as he closes his book. "Hey. You okay Boss? You look like you're limping."

Bob turns and looks at his foot as though it's the first time he'd noticed it and shrugs. "Old injury. I don't like to talk about it. Gives me grief sometimes. Have to push on though."

"What a brave guy," Colin says to himself as Bob adds an extra twist and limps towards the elevator.

"I'm Stepping-Up!" Colin calls to Gina as he struts past her desk.

"Should I requisition you a ladder?" she says glancing briefly up from her phone.

"Not that kind of stepping up," Colin giggles. "I'm getting the opportunity to improve my skills to be an even bigger asset to the business," he stops and puffs out his chest. "I'm taking over for Brenda while she's on leave."

Gina snorts, "Wow," she laughs. "Good luck with that."

"Luck;" Colin smiles, "is for the unprepared," and struts back to his desk. "How do I add something to my Career Development Plan?" he calls back over his shoulder.

Gina looks up slowly and sighs. 'As much fun as it would be to watch someone get dragged into the dumpster-fire that is Brenda's job', she thinks, and looks over at Colin... "Not that little guy," she says and reluctantly pushes herself up from her chair. "Are you sure it's something you want to do?" she asks. "Brenda's job is um..." she searches for a moment for a way to describe her thoughts on Brenda and her job; and eventually arrives at; "...shit."

Colin rubs his chin thoughtfully, "Well," he frowns, "I will admit, I'm a little concerned about her workload, but Bob has assured me it's a terrific opportunity, and will look good on my Performance Review. That's why he suggested adding it to my Career Development Pla—"

"Oh god no!" Gina blurts out. "Don't do that," she shakes her head strongly. "I fell for that once," she shudders. "Ended up stuck in a team of idiots where I considered hammering my fingers to pulp in preference to coming to work."

"Oh my gosh! That's terrible," Colin gasps. "I'm so glad you got out of *that* job."

"Who said I got out of it?" she says turning away and walking back to her desk. "I'm telling you Colin, don't add it to your Career Development Plan, you'll regret it," she wags her finger at Colin, then falls back into her chair. "Or do. What do I care?" she shrugs and turns back to her computer.

Colin rubs his eyes and wonders for a second whether he just hallucinated an entire conversation, then turns back to his own computer. "I'll make a note in the Career Development Plan, but put it in as a 'tentative'," he says to himself.

When he's done, he opens up a new meeting invitation to Brenda and types - 'Stepping Up!' in the Subject line. Then adds - 'Bob the Boss has asked me to 'step up' to look after your work while you are away on your super-fun holiday. I'm scheduling this catch-up to find out what I need to do.'

He reads it back and is worried that it might come across as pushy and adds - 'Ha ha,' at the end.

He reads it again and decides to add a smiley face just to make sure.

Because Colin the Koala knows that it's bad manners to invite people to meetings without first checking the other person's schedule, he checks Brenda's calendar to see when she has free time.

'Wow, she *is* very busy.' he thinks as he scrolls through the days. It's only Monday and her calendar is full up already. He chooses the first free spot - Friday at 10:00 o'clock, and presses *Send*.

Then sets himself a personal reminder for Wednesday afternoon to look for his VHS player.

On Tuesday, Colin checks the meeting invitation to confirm Brenda has accepted. Now that he needs to speak to her, she doesn't seem to be around anymore. 'Gosh, she must be so busy that she doesn't even have time to come and visit,' he thinks, wringing his paws together in concern. She hasn't even had time to click *Accept* on his meeting, and he feels a little uneasy about whether he is going to be able to keep up with all her work.

'Maybe Gina is right', he looks over at her playing the latest game on her phone. 'Maybe I wouldn't want Brenda's job. It must be very stressful, and if I can't keep up, it might affect my performance review,' he chews his claws and checks his email and calendar.

There's still no response from Busy Brenda. He opens the company's *Chatter* direct messaging system and can see her status indicator is green. 'Green for *go!*' he thinks and types, 'Hi Brenda! I'm excited about meeting with you on Friday at ten. I notice you haven't accepted the invitation yet. (I'm guessing because you're too busy). Is that time still okay?'

He presses the icon that looks like a mouth that means 'Send' and watches the cursor blink in the empty response field.

He chews his bottom lip and watches the cursor. Blink. Blink. Blink.

"Hi Colin," says Bob the Boss from behind him, making him jump and slide forward on the designer seat. "How are you getting on with Brenda?" Bob asks.

Colin eyes flick between Bob and the empty response field in Chatter...

Blink. Blink. Blink.

He doesn't want to make Busy Brenda look bad for not responding to him, but he doesn't want it to look as though he's not *stepping-up* either. He points to the screen to show he is contacting her but doesn't say anything.

Bob nods without reading the message, "Good to see you're on top of it, Colin," he says and calls to Graham down the corridor.

Colin watches them have a brief conversation. Graham lifts his hand to show Bob something, then continue towards Colin.

"Coffee?" Graham says, holding up his re-useable coffee cup that reads, 'No sugar for me, I'm sweet enough'.

Colin looks at Chatter again and sees her status has changed to 'Do-Not-Disturb. He gulps. "Well, I guess there's no point just sitting here waiting. It looks like I should take advantage of a break now, because I don't think I'll be getting any over the next two weeks," he grabs his own plain green re-useable coffee cup and climbs down off his chair. "But I think we'll have to go to the coffee shop downstairs. I'll need to get back quickly in case Brenda gets back to me."

"Why aren't you getting any breaks?" Graham asks as they step into the lift.

"I'm taking over for Busy Brenda," Colin says glumly, pressing the 'G' button. "She's even too busy to accept my meeting invitation for me to find out what she does."

"Ha!" Graham laughs loudly as the lift doors open.

Colin knows that Graham laughs a lot, but sometimes doesn't understand why Graham finds some things funny. Like now.

"She's not going to meet with you," Graham takes in a breath. "She doesn't *want* anyone knowing what she does."

Colin squints up at him to show he doesn't understand. "I don't understand," he explains when Graham doesn't continue.

"It's simple, she doesn't want anyone to know what she does because she hardly does anything," he says as they walk over to the coffee shop. "Haven't you noticed that she comes around at least three times a week to spend an hour telling everyone how busy she is and complaining about how lazy other people are?"

Colin rubs his chin as they join the queue behind a middle aged couple arguing over whether to order an egg and bacon roll or not.

"You can go in front," the man smiles and waves them past.

"We're good to wait, thanks anyway mate," Graham says smiling back.

"No no, you go," the man says, sneering at his wife. "I'm still deciding; apparently."

"That's very nice of you," Colin smiles up at the man.

"See?" he turns to his wife. "I told you I'm nice." He looks back at Colin. "Just the other day someone told me I was big hearted."

"It wasn't *someone*, it was your cardiologist," she sneers. "And he didn't say big. He said, 'enlarged'. That's why you can't have a bacon and egg roll."

"Whatever, you two go ahead," the man slumps and waves Graham and Colin in front of them.

"Thanks mate," Graham says turning back to Colin and mouths, "awkward."

Colin grimaces back.

"One thing I've learnt in my time Colin," Graham

continues when they are safely past the couple who are now negotiating whether a croissant is an acceptable replacement. "Is that people who are trying to cover for themselves always deflect attention away from them, by complaining about other people. And she does it all the time. So does Bob. George can occasionally, but not often. I've seen Bill do it..."

Colin reaches up on tiptoe and places his cup on the counter, "I'll have a cappuccino please," he says to the waitress with the green hair. "With extra chocolate and a long black, but not too long, for my friend."

"What's the name for the coffees?" the waitress asks writing the order down.

Colin takes a breath and speaks loudly and clearly. "Colin," he says, and turns back to Graham. "I wonder why Bob the Boss didn't ask *you* to do Brenda's job?" he says.

Graham lets out a laugh. "Mate, I've barely got time to do my own job, let alone someone else's."

Colin wonders if it would be impolite to point out that less than two minutes ago Graham had insisted that Brenda didn't do anything. "I'm worried there's going to be things that come up that I won't know how to do properly, Colin frowns. "She's got twenty years' experience, and I've only been here for a few months."

"*Twenty years'* experience?" Graham laughs. "She's *been here* for twenty years, but she's only got one year's experience; and she's repeated it twenty times. If anything, you're in front because she's nineteen years out of date."

"Coffee for Conan!" the green haired waitress calls.

"Colin?" Colin asks raising his eyebrows hopefully.

She checks and shakes her head, "Conan. Cappuccino with extra chocolate, and a long black, but not too long."

"I'll take them," Colin hold out his paws and sighs.

At 4:30 on Thursday afternoon, Colin the Koala checks the meeting invitation with Brenda again to see if there is a response, but it still reads 'None'.

He stares at the screen for a moment, then grabs his Special Reminder Notebook and climbs down from his chair.

"If anyone is looking for me," he says to Gina, "I'm

going to see if I can catch Brenda, about stepping up."

"I'll make sure to check the status of your ladder order," Gina replies without looking away from her phone.

Colin laughs, "You're so funny," he giggles and walks along the corridor. He'd never been to Brenda's desk before and isn't quite sure which way to go. Sometimes the office layout made him feel like he was on a quest to throw a ring into a volcano.

When he eventually stumbles across Brenda's desk; it's empty.

"Bugger," Colin says looking around to see if she is nearby.

"Oh. Hello," Brenda says flatly carrying several shopping bags. "So good to see you," she says in a way that makes Colin think it's not.

"Hello!" Colin says as friendly as he can.

Brenda says "Hi," again, and, "I'm in the middle of something." and, "Sorry I haven't replied to your messages. I haven't seen any of them." She walks over to her desk. "I'm looking forward to our meeting tomorrow to do the handover," Brenda smiles at Colin in a way that suggests that she very much isn't.

Colin wants to ask how she can be sorry for not seeing them or how she knows about tomorrow's meeting if she hasn't seen any of the messages, but is more concerned that The Handover is like The Macarena, and makes a note in his Special Reminder Notebook in case he needs to study up tonight.

Brenda drops the shopping bags next to her desk, to join a bizarre collection of items, including (but not limited to) a tiny chocolate wheel, a roll of bunting, five packets of candles, two unmarked boxes and three piles of pens, held together with rubber bands. He opens his mouth to ask what it all is, but before he can Brenda jumps in.

"I don't know how I'm supposed to show you how to do *everything* I do. There's just so much of it," she says, flabbergasted at her workload. "And it's important..." she leans forward and drills her eyes into Colin, *"very* important, that everything is done correctly," she leans back.

"I see," says Colin, even though he doesn't. But makes a show of writing:

Important and correctly

in his Special Reminder Notebook.

"Not like the other people around here," Brenda huffs again. "Everyone here is so lazy. I'm the one who gets overloaded because of their lack of attention to detail," she opens a document on her computer and stabs at the screen. "Look at all the changes I had to make to fix this mess," she says using the Track Changes function.

"Gosh," he says, surprised. "That *is* a lot of changes." He leans forward and peers at the screen. He can see that Brenda has made quite a lot of changes, but they all seem to be minor grammatical modifications that don't really change the meaning.

"It took me hours," she shakes her head in disbelief at her lot in life. "I've already got too much to do. But it appears I'm the only one here who seems to care about doing a good job," she folds her arms tightly and snorts in disgust.

Colin promises to pay very close attention to everything that Brenda tells him, so he can do a good job, and holds up his Special Reminder Notebook to assure her how seriously he is taking the chance to step-up. "I'm glad I scheduled an hour to run through everything," Colin smiles.

"I don't have an *hour* to spare," Brenda gasps staring intently at her computer screen. "Ha! An hour? I'd like to go home sometime. I've still got all these to finish for the week," she clicks the mouse like she's sending morse code as she opens and closes documents and checklists while rattling off a monologue punctuated by multiple "tuts" and "no time"s.

Colin tries to catch a glimpse of the documents to make a note, but they flash on and off the screen quicker than subliminal advertising. Twice he opens his mouth and raises his pen to ask a question, but isn't able to find a gap. Eventually he manages to say he will shorten the meeting to half an hour, and hopes that will be enough time for him to learn everything. "Is there anything you could send me that I can read before our meeting tomorrow?" he asks, indicating all the documents she has been opening. He knows it's always best to be prepared.

"No," she says strongly. "They won't make any sense unless I explain them," she glares over her shoulder. "You really shouldn't have left this to the last minute," and tuts at Colin.

Colin opens his mouth again to say that he has been trying to contact her all week and she hasn't responded, but before he can she starts off again.

"Everything in this place is far too complicated. No-one cares though. Look at this report," she says double-clicking to open a spreadsheet.

When it opens, she clicks through three error messages. "Then I have to manually move *this* information," she selects a range of cells, "and move them to *this* page," she shakes her head.

Colin recognises the error and smiles broadly. "I know what the problem is," he points at the screen. "I can help to fix that. If you just..."

"I *know* what the problem is," Brenda glares at him, insulted that there might be something she doesn't know. "I don't have time to fix it."

Colin points out that the problem would only take ten minutes to fix, and that Brenda probably spends five minutes three days a week dealing with the errors.

"I'd like to have ten minutes to spare," she turns back to the spreadsheet and makes some more changes before opening another one. "Then this one is *always* wrong."

Colin tries to write down the report name, but Brenda is busy explaining all the reasons why it's wrong and complicated. "It's a shame people aren't more like me and do things properly. If you're going to do a job - do it properly," she looks over at him and wags her finger. "They should teach things like *that* in school,"

Colin frowns and asks if she has spoken to the person who provides the report each week to see if they can change it for her.

"Huh, it would be nice to have the time to be able to go chatting to people," she shakes her head. "There wouldn't be any point. He won't change it."

Colin wonders how Brenda can be so sure they wouldn't change it if she hasn't ever asked and begins to shift uncomfortably from side to side.

"I need to get back to work. I know you need to get the instructions, but I'd prefer if we could do this tomorrow at the meeting we have scheduled, rather than you just dropping in." Brenda reaches down and pulls up the shopping bags she carried in earlier and drops them onto her desk.

Colin tries to point out that he had only come to confirm tomorrow's meeting because she hadn't responded, and that Brenda had been speaking ever since, but isn't able to get a chance. He watches, confused, as she pulls a range of different types of notebooks from the bags and organises them on her desk.

"Gosh. You have a lot of notebooks," he stares at them enviously.

"They're not mine," she sniffs. "Don't worry. You won't need to do this. It's just another one of Bob's requests that no-one else would have been prepared to take on, so, as usual..." she points to herself and frowns. "It's up to me."

She piles nine notebooks quickly in order of size and pushes them to one side, then empties a selection of pens from another bag into the now empty desk space. "So ridiculous. I don't know why *I* keep ending up with these jobs to do. Everyone is so lazy," she nods to herself in agreement and moves the pens around on the desk.

Colin watches curiously as she retrieves a notebook from the pile, attempts to match it with several different pens before moving on to the next one.

"That's going to have to do," she says as she matches the next pen/notebook combination. "Bob, in his wisdom, decided he wanted notebooks for everyone after he saw you carrying *that* around," she stabs a finger at Colin's Special Reminder Notebook.

He pulls it to his chest protectively and tries to ask why Bob didn't come to him, but before he can, Brenda continues.

"He said, 'just buy the same one Colin has," she laughs and waves her hand. "As though it was the simplest task in the world. I turned around and told him. Bob, I said, I don't know anything about Colin's notebook," she laughs again at Bob's stupidity, then turns to Colin. "How *could* I? I don't have your notebook."

Colin lifts his Special Reminder Notebook and starts to say - "It's just a notebook. I call it my Special Reminder—"

"Then he said," Brenda interrupts, "just get anything then. *Anything?* What does that mean? So what else am I supposed to do but go out and find a selection of different notebooks and matching pens for him to assess and approve before I can buy enough for everyone," she shakes her head again in disbelief.

Colin looks down at his Special Reminder Notebook again. "I... bought it... from the shop just across the road," he says slowly. "There's a huge pile of them near the front door," he smiles helpfully.

"*Now* you tell me!" Brenda throws her hands up in the air.

"You didn't ask me," Colin opens his mouth to say, but holds himself back. He also doesn't ask why she needed to spend time in finding so many when Bob had said to get anything.

"I'll see you tomorrow at eleven," Brenda piles the notebooks back into the bags, making it clear the conversation is over. "I've got to get all this done," she waves her hand vaguely at her desk.

"Thanks," Colin says slowly. "I'll see you at *ten* tomorrow. And I'll change it to half an hour, like you asked." Colin says.

"Yes. Ten." Brenda starts typing and tutting again. "See you then."

Colin the Koala looks around the empty meeting room. He has his computer, his Special Reminder Notebook and his coloured pens, so he can easily put the tasks into categories, set up on the table ready to go. He has everything he needs.

Everything except Brenda. He pushes down the tuft of fur on top of his head and taps his claws patiently on the table.

He checks Brenda's status on 'Chatter'. It says 'Away'.

At ten past ten, Brenda pushes the door open and drops a notepad on the table. "I thought you said we were meeting at eleven?" she says accusingly. Then smiles, sending Colin mixed messages.

Colin nods tightly and avoids saying they discussed it yesterday, and instead says, "I'm all ready to step up. I want to make sure I do a good job."

"And half an hour won't be enough time to get through everything," Brenda says making a show of checking her watch.

Colin clenches his jaw and politely points out that he had originally scheduled an hour, but then had reduced it; at her request...

"Yes, of course, I'm sure it's my fault; as usual. I've got to get back to work. I'd like to be able to actually leave and go on holiday, not have to come back on Monday. I've sent you a list of everything you need to do," she says and grabs her notebook.

Colin checks his email. "That's odd. I haven't received anything," he says scrolling through his Inbox. "When did you send it?" he looks up at her.

"I haven't sent it yet. I said I'd send it later," she checks her watch again and stands up. "I need to go," she announces and storms out.

Colin sits open mouthed for a moment and taps his paw angrily on the meeting room table. 'I need to talk to Bob the Boss,' he thinks. 'I don't want Brenda to get in trouble, but I don't want to end up not doing her job properly and looking bad.'

Colin sits at his desk and rubs his brow, wondering how to talk to Bob about Brenda, when his email program goes *Bing!* with an email from Brenda. It says she has made a list of all her work and attached it to the email.

Her email says 'People constantly come with 'Urgent Requests', so you need to be on top of everything. You never know when an 'Urgent Request' will arrive, and you don't want to be overloaded when someone needs a request completed urgently.'

Colin chews on his bottom lip and double clicks the attachment. When it opens, Colin can only see one page. He looks around to see if another one has fallen off. After he reads the list, he reads it twice more and thinks that it would only take a few hours to finish all her work each day. He worries about how many urgent requests Brenda must get that take up the rest of her time, and hopes he is going to be up to the job.

On Monday morning Colin comes in feeling tired and a ragged. He's spent the weekend worrying about stepping up, and has decided to plan his days so that he finishes Brenda's work first, to hopefully leave him enough spare time to deal with all 'Urgent Requests' that come in while he gets his own work done.

He opens Brenda's list and knuckles down to get as much done as he can before lunch.

He works hard and manages to get through all Brenda's work. He looks up and checks the time. "Is it only eleven o'clock?" he asks Gina.

"What do you mean only?" Gina replies without looking up from her phone.

"I'm finished," Colin replies.

"That's good," Gina says, with no idea whether it is or not.

"I don't know," Colin says looking back to check the list again. "I've finished all Brenda's work," he says.

"So I can cancel the ladder then?" Gina smirks.

"Finished it for the whole week..." Colin says staring off into the middle distance.

"Hi Colin," says Bob the Boss on Wednesday. "How are you going with *stepping-up*?"

"I've been very lucky," Colin says. "I made sure to finish all her normal work quickly to leave plenty of time to deal with the 'Urgent Requests'."

"What do you mean," Bob scratches his chin, "by urgent requests'?"

Colin explains Brenda's email, and how, "Most of her time is spent dealing with 'Urgent Requests' that could come at any moment and were always super-important, top-priority!"

"Uh huh," says Bob thoughtfully. "Did she happen to mention what these urgent requests were requesting?"

Colin thinks carefully for a moment. He opens his Special Reminder Notebook where he said he would write them all down to make sure he remembered them and runs his paw slowly down the page. "Gosh, no."

"I see," says Bob. "And how many of these - urgent requests - have you had to deal with so far Colin?"

Colin flicks over to the next page and scans it. "None," he nods and closes the book.

"O... kay," says Bob, spinning on his heel and striding down the corridor, "I'm just off to talk with Harold in Human Resources." He stabs the lift button with his index finger rapidly.

"Ohh. I wonder if that means Brenda is getting promoted," Colin says to himself as he walks back to his desk. "Well, whoever gets her job is welcome to it," he takes a breath and waves to Gina.

"Are you talking to me?" she asks, removing one earphone and squinting.

Colin laughs, "No I was just saying to myself that—"

"Okay good, because I'm not listening," she says pushing the earphone back into place.

"Oh Gina, always such a kidder," he laughs and walks back to his desk.

Colin Calls the Help?Desk

Colin turns on his computer and notices the background has changed. Today it's telling him it was nearly time for 'Performance Reviews and Career Planning.' He doesn't know what that means, but he thinks it sounds exciting.

He moves his mouse to open today's emails.

As always, he watches the box pop up that reads, 'Receiving your new emails,' and watches expectantly for new challenges and opportunities for the day, as the tiny green bar moves slowly to the right. He quite enjoys the tension as it inches its way across. He likes to try and guess what new emails might be hiding behind the bar, just waiting for him to find them.

Suddenly the bar stops moving and disappears.

"You didn't make it all the way across," he points at the screen.

Suddenly a new box he hasn't seen before pops up. He blinks twice and reads it. It's just one word:

Failed.

"Well that's not right." Colin says to himself and tries again. He watches the tiny green bar crawl slowly across the box until it's nearly finished and... Pop.

Failed, it says again.

Colin looks around to see if anyone is having the same problem, but everyone seemed to be working happily away.

He climbs down from his chair and walks over to Gina. She always knows what to do.

"Hey Gina," he waves and smiles. "How are you this morning?" He waits for a moment for her to answer, then realises she must be busy concentrating on her own work. "Sorry," he waves reluctantly. "I need some help. I think my email is broken and I've got a report to finish this afternoon and I need to get to my emails."

"Do I look like the IT Help Desk to you?" Gina replies without looking up.

Colin squints and peers at her closely. "I'm not sure what the IT Help Desk looks like," he says scratching his chin, "I've only spoken to them on the phone. And that was only once on my first day. But I don't think so..."

"Then why would you ask me?" she says flatly, still not looking up from her phone.

"Because you're Gina," he declares. "And you know everything," he points back to his desk, "and I've got my report to do, and my email is broken," he frowns.

"Do I look like the IT Help Desk to you?"

Colin scratches his head and wants to say, "I feel like we just had this conversation," but knows it important to always be polite.

Suddenly slaps his forehead realises what Gina is doing! Gina is being like wise old Mr. Emu.

Colin remembers the time when his teacher, old Mr. Emu, had taught them the lesson about helping people to solve their own problems instead of giving them the answer.

"Give a koala a leaf and you feed them for a day," he had told them very sagely. "Teach a koala how to find their own leaves, and you feed them for a lifetime."

Colin had never quite understood the analogy, because leaves were pretty easy to find, but he thought he kind of knew what old Mr. Emu was getting at.

'That's what Gina is doing', he thinks. 'Instead of just giving me the answer, she is asking questions, so I can learn how to solve the problem myself'.

That's it! thinks Colin. Of course! "I can find my own leaves!" he smiles. "Thanks Gina!" Colin throws his paw up for a celebratory 'High Five', but Gina is too busy with something important on her phone to notice.

He says he owes her five and heads back to his desk to dial the number he had written in his Special Reminder Notebook all those months ago.

They would know what to do. Gina had told him that the Help Desk was full of highly qualified computer experts. It had turned out that the last time he called it was also Helpful Harry's first day. When he thinks back, he remembers that even though Harry didn't *actually* end up solving his problem, he had known all about resetting passwords, plugging in to the network and sending emails.

Colin listens carefully to the menu options, because the recording tells him they have recently changed. He thinks they sound the same as the last time he called and selects option one – I have a problem with my computer and navigates the same three menus as before until a voice tells him that his call is very important to them and places him on hold.

He's secretly pleased that they have changed the hold music and replaced the uncoordinated trumpet player with a simple jingly metallic hurdy-gurdy sound.

Colin hums along to the 'ping-ping-ping' and imagines the crack IT support team; sitting patiently at their Help Desk, waiting for the phone to ring so they could solve people's computer problems.

Colin thinks it would be a difficult job to have to know everything about computers. 'They must have to study in between calls to stay up to date,' he thinks when he's startled by another recording.

"Did you know most problems could be fixed by turning your computer off and on again?" it says.

"Yes. I did know that," Colin replies. "Harry told me that last time, but thank you," he tells the recording.

He taps his feet to the hurdy-gurdy music and when the recording tells him to try turning the computer off and on again, he replies politely, "Thank you, but that didn't work," to the recording.

"Coffee?" Graham calls, holding up his plastic re-usable cup that reads, 'You can't fix stupid.'

Colin holds his paw up and strains his ear listening intently. "No," he shakes his head. "They just told me my call is important to them, and they will be with me shortly," Colin looks up at him. "I'd better stay on hold. I wouldn't want to disappoint them by hanging up," he says. "I don't know what I did to make myself so important to the Help Desk team," he says quietly covering his mouthpiece. "But I will definitely get my email problem fixed now. I need to get my report done by lunch time."

"Yeah," Graham laughs, "Good luck with that," he

says, "You should be happy if you don't end up worse off after they're done, than you were when you started," and starts off down the corridor.

"What an odd thing to say," Colin says to himself and makes a note in his Special Reminder Notebook to check what 'foreshadowing' means. "They're the experts. I'm sure they'll be able to help."

"Experts?" Graham laughs again. He seems extra happy this morning. "Sorry buddy, but they know less than you do. They're backpackers, people between jobs, or working in a run-down call centre that's been outsourced somewhere to save money."

Colin thinks it's a good idea to have a diverse group, from varied backgrounds, with diverse experiences and the common goal of helping to solve the company's computer problems.

What he doesn't know is that the only thing they all have in common is an almost a complete lack of knowledge of computers, and software. Specifically email programs.

"Hello?" a voice on the phone says. "Thank you for calling–" it begins then suddenly the line goes dead.

"Oh," Colin frowns. "Hello?" he says to the empty

phone line. "That's annoying," he huffs and redials the number.

He listens carefully to the menu options again, and worries that maybe he hadn't listened carefully enough last time, because he's sure they haven't changed.

He navigates through the series of menus and eventually gets back to the on hold music. "I hope I haven't lost my important status," he says to himself when he hears a click.

"IT Support. Edie speaking. How can I help you?"

Edie listens carefully while Colin explains his computer problem, then asks for Colin's company identification details and computer number.

"Thank you for your identification details," Edie says.

'Now we'll see some elite computer fixing action', Colin rubs his paws together quickly and leans forward. He lifts his paw over the mouse, ready to follow Edie's instructions.

"And what can I help you with today Colin?" Edie asks.

Colin explains the problem again, impressed at how thorough Edie is to double check all the facts before making an analysis.

"And am I speaking with Colin?" Edie asks.

POP! Goes the tuft of fur on Colin's head.

He confirms, that yes, he is still the same Colin as he was when he identified himself two minutes ago. And after a brief discussion also confirms that - yes, he is aware most problems can be fixed by turning his computer off and on again, and no, it hadn't fixed his current problem.

"It sounds like you're having a problem with your emails," Edie says. "I can fix that for you."

Colin turns to Gina and mouths, "They can fix that for me."

Gina stares at him disinterestedly for a moment, then looks back at her phone.

"I can see that you had a problem with your email previously," Edie says. "Your log in details had been emailed to you, but you weren't able to access them," Edie reads from Helpful Harry's notes.

Colin politely listens as Edie carefully explains how to open his email program.

Colin says that Edie's instructions were very helpful, but that isn't the problem he is having; and explains it again.

"I'm pleased I could help you with your problem accessing your email program," Edie says. "It sounds like you're also having a problem receiving emails. I can fix that for you."

"Thank you," Colin says and follows the instructions on how to receive emails, even though he knows how to do that already. And explains again, that it failed.

"Are you sure you followed my instructions correctly?" Edie asks accusingly. "Can you try it again?"

Colin follows Edie's instructions one more time and explains that he still receives the same error.

Edie says, "I will need to escalate this to second level support for you. If you don't hear from them in an hour, you can give them a call," and tells Colin to write down a special number for his 'Support Ticket'.

Colin writes down the number in his Special Reminder Notebook, and suggests maybe Edie should get a Reminder Notebook too, so it wouldn't be necessary to ask the same questions over and over.

When Colin hangs up, he leans back and imagines

Edie walking across the Help Desk floor with his ticket and patiently riding the escalator up to the level two support area and explaining the problem to them.

"All fixed little buddy?" Graham appears again, smirking.

"It's going up to a higher floor," Colin says, pointing towards the ceiling. "Must be because I'm so important to them."

"Fancy a coffee while you're waiting?"

"I thought we were getting coffee?" Colin looks up at Graham as they walk past their usual cafe across the road from the office.

"We're going to check out the new place down the street," Graham points off into the distance.

"That sounds like fun," says Colin. "What's it called?"

"It's the one the moustache guy was telling us about the other day. Doesn't have a name..." Graham laughs and shakes his head. "It just has a symbol of a coffee cup."

When the barista had told them about the cafe, Colin thought at the time that it might be confusing to find a coffee shop if it doesn't have a name to look up. But he knows he doesn't have any koala-fications in business.

Or coffee shop names.

"It must have a proper name," he says, staring up at the neon coffee cup flashing above the doorway. "Maybe I'm just too short to see it," he thanks Graham for holding the door open and heads inside. "Nice place," he stands on his tip-toes looking for a sign with a name.

"Can afford to be, with all the money they're saving on letters for the sign," Graham agrees and notices a woman with blonde hair cut into a bob, carrying three bags struggling to open the door.

When he holds the door open for her, a small boy and a girl burst past and race towards the up-cycled barber chair with the Do Not Touch sign, in the corner of the shop. The woman ignores the children and walks past Graham and Colin to place her order.

"Uhhh, you're welcome," Graham says quietly as he watches her walk to the counter. "No no, you go first. I insist," he mumbles again under his breath.

Colin steps back to avoid the twin tornadoes as they slam back into their mother's legs and begin yelling for babycinos, and almost bumps into a nice waitress with green hair and lip ring, who is picking up cups.

"Excuse me," Colin says to her. He knows it's important to be polite. "Can I ask you a question?"

"Sure," she says, scooping up the cups from the table behind them as though she's preparing to begin a juggling act. "How can I help you?"

"I'm just checking so I can tell my friends..." Colin says. "What's the name of this coffee shop?"

She smiles and points at the sign behind the counter, "It's a symbol of a coffee cup."

Colin nods. "Yes, yes. I see that," he smiles back, "but what's the *actual* name?"

"That is the actual name," The waitress laughs. "It's a symbol," she says turning back to him. "You know. Like Prince."

Colin remembers when he was at school, where it seemed more important to be taught about British history and Royalty rather than significant events that happened in Australia, so he knows there were lots of

Princes. Charles and Albert and Harry and... "Which Prince?" he asks.

The waitress tilts her head and looks at Colin as though he might be a bit simple. "The musician of course. He changed his named to a symbol."

"Who did?" asks Graham walking back over.

"The artist formerly known as Prince." The waitress looks over at Graham, who shrugs back at her.

"He sang Purple Rain, Raspberry Beret..."

"Oh," Colin nods. "*Now* I'm with you. That Prince." He makes a few twisting movements and softly sings, "party like it's 1999."

"Yes," the waitress smiles and dances along with Colin for a second. "Well. He changed his name a symbol."

Graham clicks his fingers. "Oh yeah, right. The purple guy. I like some of his stuff. Why are we talking about him?"

"I was just explaining to your little friend here how cafe doesn't have a name, is just has a symbol. Like the artist formerly known as Prince did."

Colin the Koala looks up at the waitress and scratches his head. "But isn't that what everyone calls him?"

"Calls who?"

"The artist formerly known as Prince."

"What about him?" says the waitress.

"Jesus. Are we in a playground?" Graham suddenly yells as he jumps out of the way of the two children who now appear engaged in a combination running race and screaming contest.

Colin spins around excitedly, "There's a playground?"

"*Everyone* knows who Prince is—" the blonde lady declares as one of the tiny Usain Bolts slam into her leg. "Ouch. Careful Maverick," she smiles and rubs the boy's head fondly before he screams off for lap two. "He's the purple one. He wrote that famous song about Walter the fireman."

The waitress chews on her lip ring for a moment; turns to Colin, then Graham, and then back to the woman, who waves her hand vaguely as further explanation.

"Hmm," the waitress says, her forehead creasing in what looks like an attempt to search her memory, but is actually the beginnings of a headache from the conversation. "I don't think I know that one."

The children complete lap two and begin to wage a campaign of attacks and counter attacks at each other using their mother's legs as a no-man's land. Colin is amazed how their mother is so engaged in the conversation she is seemingly unaware of the war being waged just below her line of sight.

She smiles and pushes them on their way for lap three. "Of course you do!" she rolls her eyes, "It's his most famous song. It's all about a fire, and the smoke, and the water, and when they try to put the fire out, Walter the fireman wasn't fast enough..."

Graham blinks and looks down at Colin, who can only shrug in return.

"Oh my god. I can't believe you don't know it," the woman snaps quickly. "Prince..." she says leaning forward accusingly. "You said it yourself. The purple one."

"Well, he is the purple one..." the waitress replies, "but I don't think he ever recorded a song like that..."

Colin silently mouths through the all the artist formerly known as Prince songs he knows, and raises his paw to suggest 'Raspberry Beret', when he notices the expression on Graham's face slowly arrange itself into recognition.

Graham shakes his head as though reaching a terrible conclusion. "I know I'm going to regret this," he sighs softly and reluctantly looks over at the mother. "Could you be thinking of..." he takes a breath, "*Deep Purple?*" he ventures.

The blond woman stares momentarily, then reaches her arm back and slaps Graham on the shoulder, unintentionally knocking him out of the way of the commencement of lap four. "Yes! Deep Purple. That's him," she folds her arms and nods decisively to make it clear that she had been right all along. "Told you," she glares at the waitress as though somehow the confusion was all her fault.

Graham turns to Colin and sucks in a long deep breath. "I'm a huge Deep Purple fan. Tell me the song you're thinking of again..."

"The fire song," she snaps, and huffs, to ensure they know she believes they are imbeciles. "It's about Slow Walking Walter," she says deliberately and leans her head back to look down her nose at Graham.

Graham takes a second to run through the hopeful

possibility he is wrong, "Do you mean... Smoke?" he swallows. "On the... Water?"

The blond woman's eyes narrow so tightly her face seem to become smaller.

"I know that one!" Colin calls out and sings, "Smooke... on the wa.. ter. A fire in the sky..."

The blond woman glares at Colin. "Yes. That's the one," she rolls her eyes that it took them so long. "But you'll find it's Slow walking Walter, the fire engine guy," she says crossing her arms even more tightly.

"Bah, bah, bah..." Colin crunches, playing air guitar.

"I think I'll wait outside," Graham sidesteps the racers screaming past again to the door.

Maverick takes this as the perfect opportunity to make a break for the street, but Graham is too quick, and slams the door before the tiny, screaming sprinter can escape. His mother glares fiercely at Graham through the glass and he wonders whether deep down, she was hoping the boy might escape, never to be seen again.

A few moments later Colin holds the door open for the woman as her children mount yet another attempt at liberation, even though they are clearly going outside.

"Bye!" Colin waves. "She must have a lot to do. She didn't even have time to say thank you," he calls to Graham just outside the door.

"Coffees for Graham and Callum!" The barista yells.

"Colin?" Colin turns hopefully.

"Thanks Callum," the barista pushes the cups across the counter and heads out for his break.

"What a funny lady," Colin says, taking a sip of coffee.

"Funny isn't the word I was thinking of," Graham shudders.

"Slowwww," Colin sings to himself, "walking Walte—"

"Don't," Graham flips his hand up. Then adds softly, "Just... don't."

Colin finishes his coffee and manages a sneaky glance at his watch while Busy Brenda is telling him how overloaded she is.

Again.

It's been more than three hours now since he's been able to check his emails. "I need to get to my emails to be able to do my work," he says to Brenda. "It's been three hours. I've already left four messages with the Help Desk," he taps the desk a few times. "I think I'd better call them again," he says picking up the phone and dialling the number.

"Four messages?" Brenda snorts. "I wish I only had four messages," Brenda huffs. "I have so many messages I need a filing system to keep track of them."

"Maybe you should answer some of them then," Colin mumbles to himself, remembering all the times he tried to contact Brenda when he needed to step-up, and she hadn't answered.

He points at the phone and says, "Sorry. I'm very important to them," and listens carefully to the menu options. He frowns and wonders whether he needs to tell someone that the menu options haven't changed, and eventually pushes the option for Second Level support.

A nice lady named Felicity answers the phone. Colin tells Felicity he had been talking to Edie and tells her the special Ticket Number Edie had given him.

Felicity says she doesn't know who Edie is and adds, "I can confirm that Ticket Number is resolved for you and is now closed," Felicity says. "Is there anything else I can help you with?"

"Oh," Colin is pleased, but surprised. "If it's resolved, does that mean it's been fixed?" Colin wonders how long his email had been working, and why they hadn't returned his messages. He clicks his email and stares excitedly, ready to start his day's work... Finally.

"I've got get my report done," he says to Felicity. "It was due at lunch time, but luckily Bob... He's my Boss. Said I could have an extension." Colin watches the green bar move slowly over towards the right side... "Yes..." he says leaning closer and closer to the screen as the green bar slowly fills up the 'checking emails' box. "Yes..." he hovers his mouse, ready to click the first new email of the day...

'Failed.'

Colin falls back in the chair and sighs. "It's still broken," he says dejectedly. "Why would the Support Ticket be closed is it hasn't been fixed?"

"Level One support sometimes aren't very smart," Felicity says. "But don't worry, I can fix that for you," she says and explains she will need to do something called 'remote into his computer'.

Colin had never had someone remote into his computer before, and wonders what will happen. Felicity tells him to press the 'Yes' button when it pops up to accept the remote connection.

The 'Something exciting is coming about Performance Reviews!' picture with employees smiling expectantly on his screen flashes and suddenly disappears and is replaced by a heavy, ominous black background.

Colin sucks in a breath. "Where did my friend go?" He enjoyed seeing the happy faces each morning. He calls over to Gina. "Are your happy employees still on your screen?"

I hope they're okay," he says softly, biting his claw.

Suddenly his mouse begins to move slowly across the screen on its own.

"Ah!" he screams and spins around to Gina, "My computer's possessed!"

Felicity explains that she is the one making the

mouse move as she has remotely accessed his computer. She asks Colin to show her the problem he is having, but every time he tries to move the mouse to press the email button, it jumps off to a different part of the screen as Felicity tries to do something at the same time.

"Please stop touching the mouse while I'm accessing your computer," Felicity says.

Colin wonders if it's bad manners to ask how he can show her his problem without touching the mouse. When he eventually manages to show her his email, they both watch sadly as the message, 'Failed' appears yet again.

"I can fix that for you." Felicity says and Colin sits back and watches as new windows pop open, and close again. Something called a 'Task Manager' appears and disappears.

He wonders who his Task Manager is. Probably Bob the Boss he thinks.

"Okay," Felicity says, "That should be all fixed for you now."

Colin's computer goes Bing! And he sees an email appear.

"Yay!" Colin yells. Then Bing! Another one! As more pop up into his Inbox he quickly scans them for the ones containing the information he needs to be able to create his report. He scrolls past three from Edie to say that the support ticket of Colin's emails not working was scheduled to be marked as resolved and closed, and if he disagreed, he needed to reply to say he was still experiencing the issue.

He finds the final email he was waiting for just under the survey request from Edie titled 'Don't forget to rate me highly'.

"Is there anything else I can help you with today?" Felicity asks.

"No, thank you," Colin says quickly, "Now I can add the information from the final emails I need, to the old ones, and will be able to get my report done."

He agrees that Felicity has fixed his email problem and that she can mark the Ticket as resolved and closed.

Colin beams and checks his watch. He is so grateful to Felicity for fixing the problem that he had no part in causing, so that he can start the work he should have started four hours ago, instead of making phone calls and talking to computer experts. Graham appears behind him and takes a sip of coffee.

"They fixed it." Colin says beaming. "Look!" he says, and clicks the receive button and a few more emails appear. "See," Colin points at the screen. "No 'Failed' box." Colin looks at him. "Didn't you just finish a coffee?"

Graham nods rapidly. "Alfred wanted one, so I went with him," and looks intently at Colin's screen. "Where's all your other emails?" he asks, pointing at the almost empty Inbox.

Colin stares between the screen and Graham. "I'm sure all my emails were there before Felicity fixed it. What's happened to them?" he clicks all the different menus.

"Yeah, they fixed it alright." Graham laughs, a little too manically.

"Wait," Colin says, raising a paw. "I know how to fix this," he says confidently clicking 'restart'. "Did you know most computer problems can be fixed by turning it off and then back on again?"

Graham shrugs. "I find I can fix *all* of them by just turning it off," Graham says flatly.

"Remember how on my first day how I didn't have my login details because they emailed them to me?" Colin laughs as he types his password. "If it wasn't for you, I might never have been able to start work!" he laughs again, and clicks the button to start his email program. "Phew," he wipes his forehead. "No 'Failed' message," He turns to Graham. "Looks like all's well that ends well."

Graham motions twice at the screen with his coffee cup.

"What?" Colin spins back round to the computer and sees a new message box.

'Unknown Error'.

Colin stares and blinks twice. "How can it have an error that it doesn't know what it is?" he stares up at Graham and then back to the screen. "I need to get my report done," he says as his shoulders slump and he checks his watch again. "Now I'm going to have to call them... again," he snatches up the phone. "You know," he frowns, "I'm beginning to wonder if maybe some of their crack team of experts aren't that crack after all." he dials the number and stares at Graham defiantly. "And I'm not even going to listen carefully to the menu options," he nods strongly.

Graham laughs. "Good luck again mate. Oh," Graham spins quickly back to face Colin. "Whatever you do. Don't let them do something called a Profile Rebuild," he takes another sip of coffee and shudders involuntarily. "Happened to me once. Lost everything."

Colin listens to the hurdy-gurdy again, but thinks that doesn't sound quite as perky as it has before.

When someone named Davis answers, Colin explains the new 'Unknown Error,' and how Edie and Felicity had helped him but somehow the problem is far worse now than it was the first time he called.

He verifies his identification, explains the problem again and confirms, again, that yes, Davis was talking to Colin, explains his problem for the third time and tells Davis how far behind he was with his report that was already overdue.

Davis says they don't know Felicity or Edie but tells Colin, "I can fix that for you."

Colin lets out a huge sigh of relief. "Thank you."

"I'll just need to quickly rebuild your computer profile."

Colin's eyes flick to the corridor where Graham had disappeared. "Um. My friend Graham said not to do that."

"It's nothing," Davis assures him. "All we are doing is..." he says as smoothly as he can reading from the script on his screen, "restoring some of your... system components from your black cup."

Colin looks around, "I don't have a black cup," he says. "I can check if Graham has one."

"Sorry, I meant to say back up," Davis says and adds confidently, "I do this all the time. It's a simple process."

"O... kay," Colin says. "You're the expert... I suppose," and follows Davis's instructions to log out. "I'll be so glad when this is fixed," Colin says rubbing his stomach where it feels like a small flock of butterflies has been released. "I mean, I can work on some of the report while you're fixing my email problem. It will be harder to do it that way and I'll have to redo some of it, but I'm running out of time," Colin checks his watch again. "How long will it be? Five minutes? Ten?"

"It should take no longer than 90 minutes," Davis

assures him. "You won't be able to access your computer during that time, but I will call you when it is complete and you can get straight to work. Do you have a pen to write down your Support Ticket number?" Davis asks, but Colin doesn't answer. He just stares at the phone, his right eyebrow twitching rapidly.

"Thanks for convincing me to come for a coffee," Colin says holding the door open for Graham. "I know this is your ninth coffee for the day,"

"Anything for you little buddy," he smiles. "Happy to do it to cheer up a mate," Graham says as his shoulder jerks twice. "I was a little concerned when I saw the way you were just sitting there staring at the phone to be honest," he looks over at the counter. "I just hope they haven't turned the coffee machine off for the day already."

"I can't believe it's taking so long to get a simple problem fixed. I'm getting so far behind. I'm really worried," Colin says checking his phone to make sure he hasn't missed the call from Davis, even though it's only been fifteen minutes.

"Hey Graham, back again," the waitress with the purple hair says taking his plastic re-usable cup that reads - 'Care about your environment' under the logo of a large oil company. "Usual? Long black, not too long?" she writes it down when he nods then then turns to Colin. "And what can I get for you today?" she smiles.

Colin smiles back at her. "Hi. I'll have the usual too please," he says and turns back to Graham. "I don't know what will happen if I can't get my report done. It's really stressing me out. I've never missed a deadline," he rubs his stomach to try and calm the butterflies down. "Never."

"Cappuccino, extra chocolate," she nods, writes it down and holds her pen ready. "And your name?"

Colin stares at the counter in front of him and blinks twice. "I've been coming here for over six months," he mumbles to himself. "Every day. For. Six. Months," he takes a deep breath, looks up at her and smiles. "It's... Colin. C. O. L. I. N—"

Beep! goes Colin's phone. "It's a message from

Davis," he smiles. "Maybe it's fixed already," he looks up a Graham. "I might need you to grab my coffee for me so I can race back and get started." He scrolls to the message from Davis - 'Slight problem, should be no more than another 90 minutes.'

"Sorry, what was the name again?"

Colin's arm drops and he stares up at the waitress. "It's Colin," he says stonily. "It's the same name as it was yesterday. And the day before that. And the weeks before that and months before that!" he snaps and sucks in a deep breath. "Oh! I'm so sorry," he throws his paws over his mouth quickly. "I'm having a bad day at work. I shouldn't have taken that out on you. That was very unfair of me," he pulls his collar away from his neck. "I hope you'll accept my apology," he opens up his paws towards her for forgiveness.

"Huh?" the waitress says, suddenly looking down at him. "Sorry, I wasn't paying attention. I was just reading the description of our coffee," she points at the sign over Colin's shoulder. "Bit wanky aint it?" she laughs. "Anyway, I missed your name?"

Colin sighs. "It's Cardboard," he says and slumps off to the side.

"Cheer up mate. I'm sure they'll get it sorted..." Graham taps him on the back, "...eventually. Anyway, in the meantime, think about how great it is to get paid to do nothing!"

"It would be great to get my report finished," Colin sighs. "Who wants to get paid to do nothing?"

"I think you'll find everyone wants to get paid to do nothing," Graham says.

"But don't you think it's unfair that I'm getting paid the same as Gina and Umi and George, and they're snowed under while all I've been doing all day is waiting around and drinking coffee?"

"Not sure what your point is?"

"Here's your coffee Graham," the barista calls pushing the cup across the counter. "And one for..." he checks the name, "Colin," he calls. When there's no response he holds the cup higher and calls again. "Colin?" He looks around the shop. "Cappuccino with extra chocolate for Colin?" he calls again.

"That's yours mate," Graham nudges him.

Beep! goes Colin's phone as he walks over to the counter. 'Didn't need to do a rebuild after all. All fixed!' reads the message from Davis.

Colin rubs his shoulders and stares at his computer. "Okay computer," he moves the mouse slowly over to the icon for his email program, leans down close to the keyboard, and whispers "I've got faith in you. You can do it."

He double clicks the icon, closes his eyes, crosses his claws and silently counts to ten...

"One, two three..." when he gets to seven, he carefully peeks out of one eye...

"They're back!" he yells. Plus, there's another twenty new unread ones.

Eleven are from the IT Support Help Desk asking him to complete a short survey about how happy he is about the way they solved his problem.

"Looking good?" Graham pops up behind him, bouncing from one foot to the other.

"Too much coffee today?" Colin looks over at him.

"Don'tthinkso," Graham says so quickly that all the words join together.

"All back!" Colin yells. "Now I can get some work

done."

"Yepthat'sgreat," Graham says.

"Maybe you should take a few deep breaths," Colin turns to Graham. "I'm pleased it's working again, but It seems like a lot of time and effort to just be back to where I was when I started," he shrugs. "Especially because every time they 'fixed' something it seemed cause more problems."

Graham finishes his third breath. "I've yet to head into a Help Desk call and not come out worse off than I went in," he points to the survey emails. "There's your chance to let them know what you think about their service."

"Hmm," Colin taps his chin. "I would like to ask them to stop saying they've changed the menu options when they haven't," and clicks on the link in the survey email.

A new browser window pops open and Colin and Graham watch the small icon spinning around and around and around in the middle of the page.

"Taking it's time," Graham's eye twitches and he bounces up and down.

"Gosh. It must be a big survey," frowns Colin. "I

think I might have to save this for later. I've got to get my report done."

When the icon finally stops spinning they both lean forward expectantly to the screen.

A message finally pops up that reads, 'Failed. Page not Found.'

"Maybe the Help Desk need to call themselves!" Colin laughs.

"I don't even want to think about what kind of vicious circle of destruction that would end up in," Graham shakes his head. "Probably take the entire company down," he nods and rubs his chin thoughtfully. "Hmm. I wonder how long we would get paid while we couldn't work..."

Work Smarter, Not Harder

Colin grabs his usual seat for the Friday afternoon team meeting and watches the others fill the dark meeting room. It's one of the older rooms, so even though there's a two small windows looking our into the hallway, the dark panelling on the walls suck in the light like a wood-veneered black hole.

Bob the Boss is already sitting at the end of the big table - made of four smaller tables pushed together, brow furrowed in a combination of concentration and concern.

"Gosh, I could hang my school photograph from one of those lines in his forehead," Colin thinks and nods to Graham as he sits down next to him. Graham raises his re-usable coffee cup that reads - 'Sorry. I'm all out of f*cks today', to say cheers.

Gina is fussing over her phone, scrolling back and forth showing George pictures of the new lounge her and her partner are going to buy. Colin watches the others waiting to see where Bill sits before they commit to their own position. Colin likes Bill, but agrees that he can ramble on... occasionally.

Bob calls Bill, 'Bastian' behind his back. Colin originally thought that it must be because Bob considered him a 'Bastion of knowledge'. But Graham told him it's because Bastian is the kid from the Neverending Story.

Bob glances up and waves a hand to signify - get a move on - then returns to the notes in front of him. He shakes his head very slightly so no-one can see and mumbles under his breath, "Each one of these things gets stupider than the last," and sighs.

When Bill finally chooses a seat, everyone quickly sits down like it's a game of musical chairs, before Bill has the chance to decide that 'this chair is uncomfortable' and relocates.

Bob stands up; takes a very deliberate breath, and coughs once. Umi and Pooja keep looking over George's shoulder at Gina's lounge, trying to ignore Brenda's complaints about not having time for these meetings.

Bob coughs again, slightly louder, with no success, and escalates his attention-seeking to a robust - "Ahem."

He waits for a few moments before giving up, and simply begins speaking. "Thanks," he says loudly to go over the over the cross-talk, "for coming to this important kick-off meeting today to announce that we are updating our..." he pulls the collar of his shirt away from his neck and glances around the room trying to avoid eye contact. "New Ways of Working."

"New *ways of working?*" Gina frowns looking up from her phone. "What does that mean - ways of working?"

"Are we getting more work?" Brenda glances quickly around the room. "I don't have time to take on any more work. I've already got too much to do," she huffs.

"Ways of working what?" George squints and

scratches his head.

"Our working ways?" Umi glances over at Pooja, unsuccessfully hoping she may be able to provide some kind of explanation.

"We have *Ways* of working?" asks Graham scratching his head.

"Some of us do," Bob mutters and looks back to his notes.

"Why do you keep saying, 'ways of working' instead of just 'work'?" Pooja stares at Bob like he's a five year old.

"Ways of Working," Bob forces a smile, "is simply a different, new, terminology."

"It sounds more like it's Yoda," George says and changes his voice. "Ways of working here we have," he says, and everyone laughs.

Everyone except Bob, who takes a deep breath. "Anyway," he continues, "we'll need to get used to this new terminology," he turns to Colin. "Would you be able to put together a glossary of terms for the team?"

"On it Boss." Colin gives a thumbs up and makes a note in his Special Reminder Notebook. Then adds a supplementary note to ask Bob what terms he needs to glossarise.

"Point of this, what is?" George asks, his Yoda voice slipping into more of a substandard Spanish accent.

"Alright. Thank you, George," Bob flicks him a forced smile.

"Welcome you are."

"Okay," Vanessa leans forward and whispers over George's shoulder. "You're milking it now. Let it go."

George's face drops and he crosses his arms.

Bob reads directly from the notes his Boss, Andre, had emailed him. "We are keeping pace with business best practices and moving to a more..." he pauses, shoulders tensing, "to a more... Agile, approach," then without looking up, adds, "Graham put your hand down."

Graham frowns, and lowers his hand.

Bob continues to read to tell them how Agile will bring them increased efficiency; reduced re-work and improved engagement scores.

"Agile will bring us a competitive advantage while making our time at work easier," he looks up and fakes a sincere smile. "This is a very exciting time for us as a business."

The team stare at him blankly.

"What that means," Bob says, reading from his notes again, "is that we are relentlessly searching for opportunities to improve our ways of working. Thereby driving us to be more efficient and cost-effective. We shall achieve this with the popular methodology used by many companies - known as Agile."

"I don't understand what you're saying," Umi looks around for support.

Bob looks up again at the sea of blank faces and decides it's safer to return to his notes. "Simply put," he squints at the paper. "Agile is an approach that allows us to be more, uh..." He flips the paper over and back, checks the floor as though some of the words might have fallen off the page. Unable to locate any, he straightens up and powers through. "Agile is an approach that allows us to be more; Agile, with a capital 'A', which enables us to be more agile, with a lower case 'a', in our approach."

"That didn't help," Umi frowns.

"Not following," Graham shakes his head, then

quickly adds.

Colin wants to say, "Me too," but knows he doesn't have the same koala-fications as a Bob, who would have been involved in exciting programs like this before.

"Alright. Let's get started," Bob the Boss claps his hands for attention. "This is an important initiative that will help drive us along the path to becoming a high-performing team—"

"Didn't we do this the other day with Michael and Micaela?" Vanessa calls from the back of the room. "I thought Safety said we weren't allowed to do—"

"No," Bob huffs. "This is different. It's an important step to help us on our journey to be more high-performing," he says, unsure whether he is actually trying to convince Vanessa or himself, and scratches his head.

He throws his hands up, "Look. It's very simple. It means, we get to examine the way we do our jobs"

"Why do we need to do that?" Bill asks looking at the others. "And I don't understand why you're bring up all these new terminologies and expecting us to suddenly understand what you're saying," he takes a deep breath.

Bob knows that's the signal that Bill is about to launch into a story and jumps in quickly. "I'm not springing it on you and the team, Bill. There's been an extensive communication campaign about this change," he scans his team, who stare back blankly. "Oh my god," he sighs and wonders whether he should just call it a day and leave early to beat the traffic. "It's been promoted everywhere in the office," he throws his arm up towards the corridor. "You passed two signs about it on the way to this room."

The team turn to peer out through the small window.

"You can't see them from here," Bob jumps in. "There're the ones that say 'NWOW'!"

"Oh those. I thought that was a typo," Pooja declares as the others nod in agreement.

"Yeah, me too," Vanessa agrees. "I kept wondering what 'NOW is coming' was supposed to mean. I figured it was some kind of Mindfulness thing."

"So," Bob rubs his temples. "Are you saying that you thought the company had spent tens of thousands of dollars to develop a comprehensive communications plan, engaged our entire marketing team, printed and mounted posters throughout the office, released a computer wallpaper AND screensaver and promotional items..." he squints, "and that no-one noticed an extra 'W' in the middle of the word now?"

"Sounds like par for the course to me," Graham chimes in helpfully as the others nod.

"Jesus Christ," Bob mumbles, and drops down into the chair. "NWOW;" hey says, "stands for - New Ways of Working."

"What's wrong with our old ways of working?"

"Finally, a good question," Bob nods. "There's nothing wrong with our old ways of working Alfred," he leans forward and mentally congratulates himself on his performance as an ardent support of the program. "NWOW will allow us to leverage our synergies. Streamline our—"

"In other words," Umi interrupts folding her arms, "what you are saying, is that management wants us to work harder."

Bob quickly holds up his hands. "It's not about

working *harder,* Umi," he leans forward and half closes one eye, like a lawyer about to deliver the immutable point that convinces the jury his client is innocent. "It's about working *smarter,*" he sits back and smiles.

POP! goes the tuft of fur on Colin's head.

"Are you saying I'm working dumb?" Umi's jaw drops in shock.

Colin giggles and covers his mouth.

Bob shakes his head. "I'm not saying anyone..." he glances at Brenda, "I'm not saying *everyone*, is working dumb. This initiative is..." he stares off into the middle distance for a moment, then blinks twice. "Oh for god's sake, working dumb isn't even a phrase."

He glances around the room and rubs his forehead. "Look, Agile is a well-known method to help efficiency and to increase employee engagement." He takes a deep breath and stabs his finger at them, "And besides all of you rated our processes as bad, and gave low engagement scores in the last company survey," he holds his hands up defensively. "So if you want to lay blame anywhere..." he folds his arms and sits back in the chair. "This is your own fault,"

Colin frowns and wonders if saying it's their fault is the best way to get people to want to join in, but realises that it must be a clever leadership strategy.

Alfred calls out from the back, "So this is our punishment for speaking up..."

"You're not being punish—" Bob gives up and takes a deep breath.

"For speaking up," Umi looks at him accusingly. "The way *you* told us we had to."

Bob drops his head into his hands. "I never *told* you to do anything. Look. It's well known that Agile reduces employee dis-satisfaction and increases subsequent engagement scores," he declares confidently, despite having no idea whether it's even true, let alone well known.

"Oh," Vanessa snorts. "I didn't realise it's all about how happy I am to be involved. How generous of management! Why can't they just admit it's a cost cutting exercise?"

"I don't see how punishing us with more work and less resources is going to increase engagement scores." Pooja says folding her arms.

"Easy," Graham chimes in. "Because the people

who filled out the first negative survey have bailed to somewhere else by the time the second one come 'round, and the new people don't know any better."

Bob slumps down in the chair and feels the room deteriorate into what his parents would call a 'whinge-fest'. Which is what they would call it when he would complain about their rules, like having to be home and in bed by ten o'clock on his eighteenth birthday. He checks his watch and ponders the idea of faking a heart attack to excuse himself.

"Well I think it's a great idea to look for ways to improve," Colin jumps in taking advantage of a short break in the storm of noise. "I remember my teacher Old Mr Emu would always say, 'Young Colin. There's always room for improvement.'"

Colin doesn't mention that Old Mr Emu would say that, even the times Colin had scored 100% on his tests. "I think we should give it a chance," he continues. "My friends all say they have been working Agile for ages and it's great!" and swallows uncomfortably for telling a tiny fib.

He had heard his friends mention Agile once or twice, but it usually had the word, 'fucking' in front of it.

"Thank you, Colin," Bob says and looks around the room as everyone slowly quiets down. He stops at Graham, who is leaning on the table tapping his chin. "You've been unusually quiet Graham," he sighs. "Come on, let's get it over with. What's your issue with it?"

Graham leans back in his chair and takes in a deep breath, "No issue. I think it's about bloody time," he says strongly.

"Look Graham," Bob sighs and looks back at his notes, "Okay. I know that— Wait," he flicks his head up so quickly, Colin hopes he hasn't given himself whiplash. "What did you say?"

"Yeah," Graham says nodding over to Colin, "I'm with Colin. I reckon it's about time the management spent a bit of money fixing this place up."

Colin gives Graham a thumbs up and smiles back to Bob.

"That's..." Bob stumbles. "That's... fantastic Graham," Bob smiles, then stops and glares squarely. "Hang on. Is this a lead up to some kind of—"

Graham looks around at the rest of the team, who

are all now staring at him, mouths open. "What?" he turns back to Bob. "No. I think it's a bloody great idea."

Colin watches the tension run out of Bob's body like a river in flood season.

"Well, thank you Graham," Bob says. "It's good to know I have your support." He turns to the others. "Now what about the rest of—"

"Oh yeah absolutely." Graham leans back further in the chair, causing it to let out a tiny squeak of protest, and clasps his hands behind his head. "Those Marketing and Sales teams? Pfft. They're a real bunch of cowboys."

Colin's heart jumps. "Cowboys!" he calls out. "I wonder if they know Rosebud McRae? He's my favourite rodeo rider." He straightens up and makes a mental note to visit the Sales and Marketing floor. 'This job just gets better and better', he thinks.

"And don't get me started on Finance," Graham continues. "They could definitely do with some changes. I've been saying for ages they should be more like us - efficient and professional," he glances at Brenda. "Well, like most of us." He leans forward again and shakes his head. "I'm sick of carrying them all, to be honest."

Bob pushes his thumbs into his temples again and forces out, "It's going to apply to all of us Graham, not just Sales and Marketing," Bob says and decides to throw out any pretence of interest and explains flatly, "Look. It's not optional. The entire company is doing it. And efficiency improvements and cost savings are going to be part of your Performance Review this year."

Colin taps his chin and mulls over whether it might have been helpful for Bob to have started with that.

Bob reads again from his notes and strongly reiterates that this is a significant and necessary change in the culture of the company, based on careful business analysis, the voice of employees from the company survey and countless case studies of Agile implementations in other, similar, organisations, both large and small.

"Sounds like someone in Senior Management recently returned from an Agile junket," Pooja laughs.

"No-one has been on a junket," Bob huffs

Graham's phone bings loudly, "Did anyone else just

get this email from the Hector the HR Director about the Agile conference he attended in Majorca?"

"Alright. Let's wrap it up there," Bob jumps up and quickly gathers his papers.

Colin waves to his friends, sitting at their usual table near the back of the 'What Ales Ya?' pub.

"I've got big news," he says, placing his beer on the table and climbing up onto the chair. He has a quick sip and excitedly tells them, "My company is 'going Agile'. It's going to shape the future and drive our success," he says quickly. "Our engagement scores will improve, productivity will rise, our waste and rework will plummet..." he pauses for dramatic effect, "and we'll have a more structured and robust operating rhythm."

"Ha! Lucky you," Morgan laughs.

"I know," agrees Colin. "And the best part is..." he puffs out his chest. "I've been chosen to help with the implementation in my team. My Boss, Bob emailed me about it this afternoon." Colin had been so excited that he rushed straight over to Bob's desk to 'bounce some ideas around', but Bob must have been in an important meeting somewhere because Colin couldn't find him.

He has another sip of beer and smiles, thinking about how he will be instrumental in helping the company succeed.

"Yeah," Morgan says, taking a gulp of his own beer. "We had a big efficiency initiative like that at our place last year. One of those big consulting companies came in and spent months charting how our processes worked, creating these huuuuge process maps on the walls next to the places where we would actually perform the task so we could follow the process along as we were doing it," he takes another gulp of beer. "That way we could compare what was supposed to happen to what actually happened and identify gaps and improvements."

"Wow," Colin gasps, imagining everyone crowded around a giant process map, pointing to places that it could become more streamlined. High-fiving each other when someone spotted a wasteful step to be removed. "What happened? How many efficiency gains did you find?"

Morgan shrugs and finishes his beer. "I think we had one... na, maybe two meetings standing in front of it, but that was it. The consultants came back a couple of times and added some random arrows, then disappeared. That was..." he looks up trying to remember. "Maybe six months ago," he slaps his hands on his thighs and stands up. "My shout," he says heading towards the bar.

"Wait. What?" Colin sits back on the stool. "That can't be the end of the story," he looks around at the others. "What improvements were there? What efficiencies were gained? How much did morale improve?"

Morgan rubs his top lip and thinks for a moment. "Well, someone wrote 'bullshit' on the process map in red pen, and then later someone else drew a dick and balls. I suppose that increased their morale a bit."

Colin closes his mouth and takes a deep breath. "But... but surely there were improvements to the processes... wasn't there?"

"Last week half of the process map fell off the wall."

Colin frowns and looks down into his beer. "Well,

I'm sure ours will be different," he mumbles.

His friends pat him on the back and tell him they're pleased he's involved, because it will look good on his resume. But not to get too excited. Realistically no-one in his team was going to be interested. And for the most part would be hoping that - like previous efficiency initiatives - management would soon get bored of it, and would replace it with the next latest business fad.

"Well," Colin insists, "maybe in your company, but I work with a committed team of go-getters, steered by a dynamic leader, with a passion for business improvement, team engagement and shareholder value that helps drive us into the future," he says and stares back into his beer trying not to think about the team meeting...

"Happy Monday," Colin calls breathlessly to Gina as he rushes past. "My bus ran late this morning. I can't believe it happened on the big day."

"Big day?" Gina reluctantly pulls an earphone from

her left ear.

"It's our first agile introduction session," Colin puffs, throwing his bag down and snatching up his computer.

"Oh. Right," she rolls her eyes and pushes the headphone back in.

Colin rushes down to the big meeting room where Bob is already setting up.

"Sorry I'm late Boss, my bus was stuck in traffic," Colin puffs again as he swings though the door. He feels honoured that Bob has chosen him to help and doesn't want to put his position in jeopardy. "It won't happen again."

Bob waves it away magnanimously without mentioning that he had arrived only a few seconds before Colin because he'd overslept.

Colin jumps back out of the way as Bob pushes the tables together and heads past the two desk chairs Bob has wheeled in and placed at the front. 'We must be having guests' Colin think to himself, and moves to the whiteboard to check the markers are working. "I'm really looking forward to finding out more about agile," he says drawing lines on the board and dropping four of the five markers into the bin. "I'll go and grab some more pens," he says and smiles. "Those ones," he points to the bin, "are... unre-mark-able," and giggles.

Bob laughs in spite of himself and says, "Okay great. Sorry I haven't been able to share much information with you, senior management wanted it on a strict 'need to know' basis." Which in reality meant that Bob had forgotten to send Colin the information.

Colin nods and touches the side of his nose to show he understands the secrecy, then heads off to see Sergei for some new markers. He bounces along the corridor, chuffed at his role to help 'drive the way the company operates into the future', and waves as he walks up to Sergei's desk.

"Hey Sergei, how are you today? Could I get some whiteboard markers for the big meeting room please?"

"Hello Colin," Sergei smiles. "Of course," he pulls out a pack of four new markers.

"Thanks," Colin says reaching for the packet.

"Where are the old ones?" Sergei pulls back the markers before Colin can grab them.

"Uh," Colin looks back toward the meeting room. "I threw them in the bin."

"You don't have old pens?" Sergei asks, narrowing his eyes. "I can't give you new pens unless I see the old pens," he says pulling the packet further away. "Those are the rules."

POP! goes the tuft of fur on the top of Colin's head.

"Uh... Oh sorry, I didn't know you needed them. I threw them away," he tilts his head to one side. "Is there a special recycling program for them?" he asks, thinking he will go back to the room and retrieve them, so he doesn't damage the environment.

"No," Sergei laughs. "They're toxic. I throw them in the bin."

"Oh. Well, I've saved you the trouble," Colin's smiles feeling better. "I already threw them in the bin," and reaches out his paw for the new packet.

Sergei shakes his head. "I need to see the old ones."

"Uh... why do you need to see the old ones?" Colin scratches his head.

"How do I know that you really threw away the marker pens?"

"Um..." Colin furrows his brow, "because... I just *told* you that I did?"

"Ha!" Sergei laughs sarcastically. "Anyone could come by and say they had done that, and just ask for more markers," he pauses, "or pens, notebooks, staplers."

"Has anyone ever done that?" Colin tries to smooth out the tuft of fur on his head.

"No," Sergei nods confidently.

"Then—"

"Because they know that Sergei knows the rules, and will not give them new stationery without seeing the old one."

"But," Colin frowns, "why would someone come to get new marker pens... if they didn't need them?" Colin asks.

"Who know?" Sergei shrugs. "People are weird."

Colin glances over his shoulder and says, "Okay, I suppose I can rush back and fish them out of the bin," he checks his watch and grimaces. "I'll have to run."

"Meh. That's fine," Sergei says waving Colin's offer away. "I trust you Colin," he smiles and holds out the markers.

By the time Colin gets back, after a brief stop in the toilets to comb his fur back down, half the room is full of people he doesn't know. He stops and looks back out the door thinking he maybe came back to the wrong room. He looks around for Bob and rushes over to ask what was going on.

Bob adjusts his collar as he glances around and gulps. He explains that for this Kick-off meeting, they've combined a few different areas - to make it more efficient.

Colin smiles, "We're already agile, and we haven't even started yet." He places the markers carefully into the tray on the whiteboard and leans down to retrieve the old markers from the bin to return to Sergei, even though he had said he didn't need to.

Mrs Wombat had always said, "If someone believes you are trustworthy, it's always important to prove them right."

He slides the old markers into the now empty packet and waves at his team as they meander through the door.

Colin glances around at the other people, wondering where they are from and what they do. Some look very important. He sees the hungry lady from the TV in the meeting about having too many meetings, and waves and opens and closes his mouth a few times.

"Who's that lady behind Bob?" George points and asks as Colin as he walks past.

"Fifty bucks says she's a consultant," Vanessa says out of the corner of her mouth.

Colin looks back at the lady sitting behind Bob. She must have come in while he was grabbing the new markers. He thinks she looks like a friend of Bob's who's dropped in on her way to from the gym, because she's dressed in yoga pants, an exercise shirt and runners.

"Thanks for coming," Bob begins softly as the final stragglers find a seat. He coughs once and tries again, reading from the same notes as Friday's team meeting without looking up.

"... therefore, this initiative allows us to examine our current state, align to our purpose, and implement improvements. It is a valuable opportunity for all of us as an organisation to take a step back and to refocus." Bob pulls his collar away from his neck and clears his throat, again. "Which will allow us to identify cost-savings and efficiencies," he looks up finally at the group. "Any questions so far?" he reluctantly asks.

"Who's that behind you?" Graham asks pointing over Bob's shoulder.

"I expect she's from Personnel," Bill replies confidently, "to deal with the all the inevitable redundancies."

"Redundancies?" George spins around while the rest of the room begins to mumble amongst themselves.

"Looks like it was a quick decision to invite her too," Bill says. "They didn't even give her time to get changed into her work clothes."

George looks between Bill and the lady, trying to remember if he has seen her before. Her face doesn't ring a bell, and he raises his hand, his large arm blocking the view of two people behind him.

Colin smiles. He is always impressed when someone raises their hand to ask a question. It's very good manners.

"Yes, you have a question, George?" Bob acknowledges him, then remembers Friday's meeting, "that isn't not Yoda related?"

"When you say 'cost-saving and efficiencies',"

George frowns, "is that just..." he looks over at Bill, who nods in support, "code for 'Redundancies'?"

Bob shivers as he feels the air in the room suddenly grow still and cold. He's sure that he will be able to see his breath when he answers. "There's no reason to be concerned about redundancies," he says carefully. "Any redundancies will follow the company's well practices processes, as they always do," he tries to say nonchalantly to remove some of the tension, but only makes it worse. "It's not like anyone is going to be asked to pack up their things after this meeting," he laughs then grimaces.

Colin checks in his pencil case to see if he has any heartburn tablets, because it looks like Bob could use them.

"Redundancies?" a shrill voice calls out from the back causing Colin to jump. "No-one said anything about redundancies."

Bob waves his hand down to say, 'calm down' and says, "I'm not aware of how any redundancies will be determined," then realises what he has said and quickly adds, "or even if there will be any."

Gina quickly opens her phone and texts her

partner, "Don't buy the lounge!"

"But I've just taken out a mortgage," Pooja says, eyes wide.

"My job's too important to make redundant," Busy Brenda grunts and crosses her arms tightly.

"I've been through this before. They make you do practice interviews for your next job," a thin man with a bow tie declares.

"I don't want to have to do practice interviews," Vanessa turns to Alfred, breathing rapidly. "I hate practice interviews."

Bob rubs his temple with his thumb as the noise increases, "God give me strength."

"Oh, no," Alfred smiles back. "I find practice interviews exhilarating."

"I think—"

"Alright. Stop!" Bob throws his hands up him to mime 'stop', in case his verbal 'Stop' had been somehow ambiguous. "Look, it's way too early to be talking about this. I'm sure in other companies, it hasn't led to redundancies," he says, looking sideways at the woman behind him for support and receiving none. "We haven't even decided what processes to look at yet."

"I know someone on the eighth floor," the shrill woman from the back calls out, "who knows someone who works on the fifth floor near Procurement and Purchasing, and they said they know someone who has already been made redundant," she folds her arms and nods confidently.

Bob pushes his thumb into his temple, slightly concerned about how far it sinks in. "Okay," he begins slowly, wondering if his voice sounds a bit odd. "First of all, I know who you're talking about and it wasn't a redundancy," he pauses for effect. "It was a retirement. Secondly," he looks directly at the woman. "Procurement *is* Purchasing," he listens to his voice again, concerned he may have pushed his temple too hard. "And it's just called Purchasing."

"See!" she yells, causing several people to block their ears. "They've already gotten rid of the entire Procurement team!"

"Listen," Graham lifts his hand high and waits until the noise settles down. "If it benefits others, I'm happy to take one for the team and accept a redundancy to reduce our numbers."

Colin sits back in the chair. "Gosh. That's very generous of you," he salutes Graham to show how impressed he is at his offer to sacrifice himself for the benefit of his team-mates.

"Yes. Very altruistic of you Graham," Bob says flatly, "but redundancies don't work that way. Redundancies aren't about reducing headcount. They are about the job role, not the person. Your role is redundant when your position is no longer necessary, and the company can run effectively without you."

"Exactly," Graham nods. "I've got twenty years of information sitting back there," he points over his shoulder with his thumb." You can use them for the future," he folds his arms smugly. "Make me redundant. You could do this without me."

"That's true," agrees Bob, "but it's not what I said." He takes a deep breath and tries to bring the meeting back on track. "But it doesn't matter," he says strongly, "because there *aren't* any redundancies."

"This reminds me," Bill pipes up loudly, "of the redundancies we had years ago..."

"Oh God no," Bob drops back into the chair and pushes both thumbs against his temples again as Colin sits up straight to show he's listening.

Colin enjoys Bill's stories. He always thinks it's funny how everyone tries to avoid Bill when they are at their desks, but always encourage him to talk in meetings. Colin thinks that's probably so everyone gets to hear the story.

"I remember years ago," Bill begins, looking up into air. "There was this young man, Andrew something-or-other, his name was," he pauses. "Back in my day, they offered voluntary redundancies..."

"Back in your day they still used carrier pigeons." Brenda snorts.

"Anyway, this young lad... Andrew... Carpenter. Yes. Carpenter I believe his name was. He used to work on the seventh floor," he laughs. "Oh I can tell you the seventh floor was very different back then," he laughs to himself.

"Is this still the same story?" Vanessa whispers to George, who shrugs and watches as Bill tilts his head up again, thinking about the young Andrew Carpenter.

In the silence Colin hears a faint ticking. He scans the room and realises it's the woman at the front tapping her watch with a pen at Bob.

"Yes, well, as I say," Bill suddenly begins again, "Andrew Carpenter registered for a voluntary redundancy you see—"

"Let's move it along please," Bob says staring at the carpet knowing full well that Bill won't move it along, or stop until he's ready. Or until everyone has walked away.

"I think we should let him finish," the shrill woman calls.

"Yes. A voluntary redundancy. Then young Andrew became very angry when his redundancy came through and he had to leave," Bill laughs.

Colin laughs as well to be polite, but isn't quite sure why.

"Uh," Pooja scratches her head, "I don't get it."

Bill leans forward to deliver the key point he realises he'd forgotten to add, "He was angry because he expected his Manager to fight to keep him," he shakes his head. "He said - it was just a test!"

"Ha!" Graham laughs. "If he volunteered for redundancy, what did he think was going to happen? It's not hard to work it out. It's in the word... Re-done-dancy," he snorts, "you're done, mate."

"Yes," agrees Bill. "He really should have thought it through..." and falls silent.

A woman behind Colin raises her hand and says, "I'm sorry. I'm not sure of the purpose of—"

"Oh don't even try." Bob slaps his hands on his knees and stands up. "Okay, let's get back on track—"

"He said he did it as a test!" Bill bursts out laughing, shaking his head slowly in disbelief as though it was the first time he'd heard the story of Andrew Carpenter's redundancy.

"See," Graham points at Bob accusingly. "That's what a good manager does. Doesn't stand in the way of his employees getting the redundancy they deserve."

Bob stares at the ceiling and takes another deep breath, partially to calm himself and partially willing the ceiling to collapse on him. "Let me be very clear," he stares directly at Graham. "There. Is. No. Talk. Of. Redundancies."

"I bet that's what they said before they cannon-balled Procurement," someone calls out.

"That's right," agrees Brenda. "Maybe if *they'd* had a Manager that stood up for them, all those poor people would still have jobs."

Bob runs his hand through his hair and frowns at the strands that come out in his fingers. "Look..." he says very slowly and carefully. "I'll say this one more time," he pauses. "No-one in Procurement..." he looks at the half angry/half confused faces and shakes his head. "Forget it. Let's please, just get back to the purpose of this meeting."

Colin makes a note in his Special Reminder Notebook to mention to Bob that he noticed his good manners in saying please.

"Sure, go ahead. We can take my redundancy offline," Graham motions for him to continue.

Before Bob can, Colin is distracted by a tall blond man wearing running shorts and a t-shirt trying to sneak into the room.

He's very tall and athletic. He moves fluidly sideways through the door, bumps into a table which almost knocks a glass of water onto the floor, and then slowly drags a chair across the floor to place it next to the woman, making a 'thump-thump-thump' sound as the legs bounce off the carpet.

Bob turns around and waits for the newcomer to get settled, "Can I..." he raises his eyebrows.

The man gives him a thumbs up, rolls the empty desk chair out of the way and plonks his chair next to his gym attired colleague. He quickly spins it around backwards and drops down onto it heavily, leaning forward over the backrest.

"Right," Bob turns back to rest of the room. "The purpose of today is to kick-off our agile implementation and introduce you to the two agile coaches who are going to support us."

"They do look quite agile," Graham says to Colin

"Explains the gym outfits," nods Colin.

"This is Kym," Bob checks his notes and looks back at the two visitors, "and..." he double checks his notes and looks back at the visitors. "Are you both named Kim?" he whispers. The man's eyes widen, and he turns to his colleague and smiles, "Oh yeah. We are too!" and raises his hand to high-five her.

"Kym, and, Kim work for one of the big consulting firms," Bob says turning back to the audience again.

"You owe me fifty bucks."

"Shut up, I do not."

"Jesus Christ," Bob mutters. It's like teaching a fifth-grade class." He speaks up again. "The... Kim's are going to be our agile support people. There's several of them across the whole company to help us."

"Ah." Colin nudges Graham, "You were right. That group we saw on the way back from coffee wasn't a mixed-gender basketball team after all."

Kim lifts his hand off the backrest of his chair and motions to Kym to indicate 'After you.'

"Thank you Kim..." she stands dramatically, causing her desk chair to roll backwards and bang into the portable flip chart holder with a clunk. "And thank you for the introduction Bart," she finishes, ignoring the clatter of the markers rolling out of their holder and onto the floor.

"Bob."

"Of course," she replies.

Colin notices Kym is also quite tall (although to him everyone is quite tall) as she struts to the centre of the room. He's impressed at how professional, smart and crisp she appears, even wearing gym clothes. He can tell she is all business.

Kym provides a brief introduction to New Ways of Working, and explains, "They are based around the Agile (with a capital A) methodology. Operating within this framework will allow you to be more agile (lower-case a) in your work."

Colin smiles at the distinction. It reminds him of his time with Mrs Wombat learning all about big letters and small letters.

It sounds like Kym was working hard to learn her letters, so Colin smiles and nods to show that he's being supportive.

When she goes on to say that many companies are moving to Agile for their projects and that waterfall is on the way out, Colin frowns. He likes waterfalls! 'I need to check the news more often,' he thinks and makes a note in his Special Reminder Notebook, and also adds a note to call Mr and Mrs Crocodile to make sure they have enough water.

"A foundational pillar of Agile," says Kym, "is the Stand Up."

Colin looks up from his notebook and shifts excitedly in his chair. 'Maybe I could get a turn at doing stand-up to tell my new joke,' he thinks, 'What do you call a fake cat? An Impusster!' He smiles and is sure he can hear a faint 'Boom-Tish'.

"The Stand Up," Kym continues walking from one

side of the room to the other, "is all about making meetings more streamlined, efficient and user-friendly. You all know that you'll be much happier and more productive having these dynamic fifteen minute meetings standing up, instead of having to guzzle coffee to stay awake through whatever meetings you currently have," she waves her hand dismissively to indicate the stupidity of the current meeting regime. "What meetings do you have Bart?"

"It's Bob. And we have an hour team meeting on Friday afternoons. But they're not bor—"

Kym waves her arms in a flourish like she's just completed a magic trick. "My point exactly. An hour a week?" she says and opens her mouth in mock surprise. "Stagnant. Old news. Out the door," she points toward the door and everyone turns their heads. "No more sitting around drinking coffee listening to this guy ramble on," she laughs and points her thumb at Bob, then adds a knowing wink.

A few politely laugh back, even though most of the room have no idea who he is.

Before Kym can continue her monologue about stand-ups, she is briefly side-tracked by a discussion where she confirms that, yes, they are permitted to have coffee at a stand up, but no, they're not permitted to sit down while they drink it; because the stand-up is about being dynamic. She slaps her hands together twice to demonstrate the dynamic nature of a stand-up and explains that each person has a specified number of minutes to talk about any issues they are having, what they did yesterday, and what they are planning to do today.

"In my day we called that 'micromanaging'." Bill leans over and whispers to Umi.

"In your day they sent children into coal mines." Umi whispers back.

Colin thinks that sounds like a pretty terrible holiday, especially for children, while Kym continues to explain that the fast-pace of the stand-up also addresses the concerns that were identified in the series of meetings HR ran to understand why people felt they were spending too much time in meetings.

She forces a smile that looks like it has been carved from granite and looks around the room as though she is though daring anyone to disagree, before turning to her counterpart, who hasn't moved from his chair.

He nods enthusiastically and adds, "A nimble fifteen-minute stand-up each day is far more efficient than a boring one-hour meeting," he declares.

POP! goes the tuft of fur on Colin's head.

He lifts his paw and counts off the number of minutes that five, fifteen-minute meetings add up to.

Twice.

And scratches his head.

"Oh, well that's very good," nods Pooja. "I don't really like the weekly meetings. They tend to drag on. No offence Bob," she adds quickly.

"That's excellent!" Kym yells so excitedly Colin feels as though he needs to High-Five someone. "No more boring meetings taking up all your time. Just your daily stand-ups, and weekly scrums."

"Scrums?" a man in a pinstripe suit asks.

Colin raises his paw. "I'm too small for football," he says. "The last time I played rugby, the opposite team kept thinking I was the ball."

"Don't worry little guy. It's not football," Kim calls from his chair, "Scrum is an Agile name for weekly planning sessions."

"How long do these scrums go for?" Pooja asks.

"They're very strictly timed to only one hour." Kim declares.

"Yes, you have a question. The man with the re-usable coffee cup that says, 'Kill me'," he points to Graham. "Gary, was it?"

"Graham," Graham replies. "I'm not a mathematician," he says in such a way that it sounds like he's suggesting that's exactly what he is, "but it seems to me that instead of spending sixty minutes a week in one team meeting, we're going to be spending," he does a quick theatrical addition on his fingers, "two hours and fifteen minutes, in six meetings—"

"I'll stop you there," jumps in Kim, holding up his hand as though he's stopping a train. "You're thinking of the 'Old' Ways of Working. These aren't 'meetings', Gary. They're 'Agile sessions.' Stand-ups, scrums, retros, and the scrum of scrums are the—"

"I'm sorry," interrupts Graham, "the what of what, now?"

"The Scrum of Scrums," Kim replies making it clear that it is an obvious, easily grasped concept.

Colin giggles quietly to himself and mumbles,

"Scrum-a-dum."

"...it's when all the Scrum Masters get together to discuss..."

Vanessa looks around the room. "Sorry. Have I been teleported to an alternate Dungeons and Dragon's Universe? I feel like I should have been issued a sword, or a stone, or something..."

Bob checks his watch, annoyed that it's already past his allocated donut time. "Looks like we've run out of time," Bob declares and stands up before things can slide any further off track. "Let's wrap it up for now. Can my team hang around for a minute?" He says and claps to signal the session is over. "Thanks Kym and... Kim. We're excited to have your support," he says as everyone files out of the room; exponentially more confused than when they walked in.

"Thanks yourself," Kim pushes himself up off the chair causing it to tip over. He steps over it and walks over to Bob. "I'm Kim," he says holding out his hand and smiling. "I didn't catch your name?"

"It's Bob," Bob says very deliberately.

"Great job on the session today Bart," the man in the pinstripe suit calls as he leaves.

"Hey Bart," Kim squeezes Bob's hand, "great to meet you."

"I'm the lead, and Colin here is going to help out on the implementation as well," he motions to Colin.

Colin waves 'Hi' and says, "I'm looking forward to being agile," and bounces from side to side to show he's ready. "I'm with Bob the Boss 100% and he's behind this 110%. So get ready to work with the most agile team you've ever worked with!"

"That's what I like to hear," Kim high-fives Colin and Bob. "Looking forward to working with you Craig and Bart, love your commitment," he says noticing another agile consultant walking past. "Gotta run," he says quickly rushing to catch up with them.

"He's really full of energy," Colin says to Kym as the rest of the team assembles.

"Yes. He is," Kym agrees. "I wanted to let you know that Kim and I will be rotating through different teams, so I'll be with you for your first stand-up on Monday and then you'll be on your own until Kim joins you on Thursday," she smiles and heads out of the room.

"I can't wait to get started in our first stand-up,"

Colin says, "and to learn more about the other agile things that make a difference, aside from meetings."

"I think this can actually be helpful," Alfred agrees, "I've worked in a few places that were agile. The tools are rather useful."

"Yeah. I've heard a few good things too," agrees Pooja as Colin covers his mouth so no-one sees him giggling at the word 'tools'.

"Yes, while it's going to require a different mindset, and the terminology is a bit childish, it is actually discipline that can have a great impact on how we work," Bob concurs.

"Do we really need to stand up if she's not around?" George asks.

"Ha! No of course not," Bob snorts and picks up his notepad. "Let's get back to it team," he says and waves for them to follow him to the door.

"When do we hear about the redundancies?" Graham asks, still sitting in his chair.

Colin covers his mouth again, but this time because now Bob looks like the hungry baby bird. His mouth just keeps is opening and closing and opening and closing. But nothing is coming out.

"I need a coffee," says Graham and heads off to grab his '#sorry, not sorry' re-useable coffee cup.

"I need a drink," says Bob.

"I need some lunch," says George.

"I need an ending," says Colin, wondering how to finish the story.

ELWOOD SCOTT

Always Give 110% Koala

Bing! goes the reminder on Colin's calendar at five minutes to three. He's not sure what the meeting is about, only that it's a presentation about changes to the Performance Management process. Colin doesn't know what the old process was, but he's always excited to hear about something new.

"Safety First," he says making sure to lock his computer screen before he climbs down from his designer chair. He stretches and rubs his lower back, grabs his Special Reminder Notebook, and heads off towards the big meeting room.

"Hi Colin," Alfred waves as he steps into the lift. "I'll hold the door for you," he smiles and places his hand across the sensor.

Behind him, the two marketing people glare at each other and fold their arms tightly.

"Thanks for your patience, just holding the lift for my buddy," Alfred says over his shoulder.

The marketing people wave back at him, "Yeah. All good. No rush," they say and smile, until Alfred turns back around.

"Everything okay Colin, you're a little slower than usual?"

"Yeah, my back's been acting up again. Not sure why," he rubs a spot just to the left of his hip. "My friends say it might be something called 'ergonomics', to do with bad chairs and non-adjustable desks, but I told them that we have very expensive designer furniture and a brochure about how to set up your chair, so it must be something else." He points at a poster of a burglar looking at a computer screen and rubbing his hands together as the lift doors close. "Did you all remember to lock your computer screens before you walked away?" he asks playfully. "I did," he smiles proudly. "Safety First," he says and rubs his back again.

"We're going to the big meeting room," Colin turns to the marketing people. It's my favourite room. Do you ever use the big meeting room?"

"We use it all the time," they say. "It's just a meeting room."

"It's the meeting room where everyone has the most fun," Colin says, holding the lift door open for them before they start walking down the corridor. "There's always silly drawings and funny made-up words written on the big whiteboard wall. He looks through the big window as they come up to the room. "See," he points excitedly at where someone has written 'Frenemy' and drawn two stick figures. "Frenemy..." he laughs and shakes his head, "You must have such a good time."

"Frenemy isn't a made-up word," the marketing people say together, "It's a friend who's an enemy," they snap striding off.

"Sounds made up to me," Alfred says.

"A friend... who's an enemy..." Colin giggles again looking around for an empty chair. "Those marketing people are so silly."

"We'll give it another minute then we'll start," Bob

calls from the front of the room and has a quick bite of a donut. "Uh, everything okay over there Colin?" he says, looking over at the little Koala trying to cover up his laughter.

"Yes," Colin tries to collect himself and points to the whiteboard, "Sorry. Alfred and I were just talking to some marketing people about 'frenemies'. Do you know what a..." he giggles again, "a frenemy is?"

Bill scratches the back of his head and thinks for a moment. "If I'm not mistaken the piece of the foreskin that joins to the base of the penis—"

"Jesus Bill!" Bob yells. "What is wrong with you? You can't say that. Harold from Human Resources will be here soon."

"What's this meeting about?" George leans over and whispers to Vanessa as she sits down in front of him.

"I'm guessing it's going to be HR telling us how they're going to screw us out of our bonus again this year," she stage-whispers back. "While making out it's somehow for *our* benefit."

"No-one is going to be screwing anyone," Bob says, placing his donut back in the box that reads, 'for being a great Boss' on the lid. "Maybe this is a good opportunity to quickly revisit our company values while we wait for Harold," jumping up and grabbing a marker.

"Is punctuality one of them?"

"To begin," Bob says over his shoulder as he writes on the wall.

Colin raises his paw to point out the handwritten sign that reads - 'Not a whiteboard! Do not write here!' next to where Bob has written VALUES in capital letters.

"We can talk about frenemies later Colin, for now, who can tell me what our company values are?" He raises his marker and steadies himself to keep up with the answers he knows will need to capture.

Colin notices the tick-tock of the clock at front of the room. At some point it's slid down slightly to the right, so the 12 is where the 1 should be. Behind him, someone plays a 'cricket' sound on their phone.

"Alright everyone," Bob huffs. "It's not that hard—"

"That's what she said!"

"That'll do thanks Graham," he swings back to the group and asks loudly. "Think about our business.

Think about what we stand for as a company," his eyes move slowly across the room, connecting with each team member. "Our values are what are important to us a business. Think about what's important to our Senior Executives?"

"Profit."

"Screwing over employees."

"Pretending that changes are to benefit us instead of admitting that—"

"Sorry I'm late..." a voice booms across the room.

Colin jerks his head toward the source of the sound that's echoing throughout the room and sees a man filling the doorway. Colin looks at the place he would normally look to see a person's face, but it's not a face, it's a chest. He scans up, past a red bow-tie, and keeps going until he has to rub his neck because it's tilted so far back. "It's a giant," he mouths silently, his jaw dropping slowly.

"That's okay," Bob smiles. "I was just taking the team through a quick activity. You know how it is. Sometimes they just need a bit of leadership to pull them in the right direction to get started."

Harold puts up his hand, "Don't let me stop you,"

he booms. "What is the activity?"

Bob points to VALUES on the wall. "As you are kindly speaking to us about the changes to the Performance Review system, I thought it would be a good time to revisit our values," he narrows his eyes at Vanessa, "so that everyone understands the company is here *for* the employees, not against them."

"Please, go ahead," Harold waves for Bob to continue. He checks his watch and pulls a chair off to the side. "We can take about 5 minutes."

Colin watches as Harold sits down, he keeps lowering and lowering and lowering, and then seems to fold himself somehow so that his knees don't bump into his chin.

"Plenty of time," Bob turns back to the wall, marker ready. "Now we're at a bit of a block, because I'm guessing it's hard for the team to *consciously* think about them," he pushes his shoulders back, "because they see me living them every day. It's just part of the culture within my department."

"Of course," Harold agrees, even though he's not sure what Bob is trying to say.

"Okay everyone," Bob turns back and spreads his

arms wide. "Now I want you to think about how you see me acting every day. What are the values that I live and embody..." he waits, pointing at his chest.

"Micromanaging?"

"Stealth donuts?"

"Taking credit for other people's work—"

"Yes, ha ha," Bob says flatly. "You're all very funny, but this isn't the time for jokes."

"What jokes?" Gina whispers to Vanessa.

Colin quickly raises a paw to cover his giggle.

Bob turns back to the wall, underlines - VALUES and steps back. He taps his chin twice, steps forward, adds a second underline, contemplates a third then nods definitively, as though he has just filled in the final pieces of the puzzle that will lead the team to enlightenment.

"What about the ones on the wall over there?" Graham calls out, pointing to the poster on next to him that contains the company vision, mission and values beside a photograph of a supportive and smiling CEO. Colin squints and can see that someone has given him a tiny goatee and moustache.

Bob spins around and hides his surprise. "Yes.

Well spotted Graham," he quips. "I was wondering how long it would take for someone to notice that. "As you were the first to see it, would you like to read out the first value please for the group?" Bob smiles at Harold and folds his arms lightly.

"Not really."

"Uh. What do you mean – not really?" Harold asks, raising his eyebrows.

Colin thinks it almost makes him tall enough that he would have to duck to leave the room now.

"Well," Graham says leaning forward, "Bob asked if I would like to read out the first value," he looks around the room, "I'm pretty sure everyone here," he winks at Gina, *"almost* everyone here..."

Gina scowls and scratches her nose with her middle finger back at him.

"...can read. So, thank you for asking if I'd like to, but no thanks," he leans back in the chair and slides forward awkwardly on the sloped designer seat.

"I'd like to do it," Colin says raising his paw. He would always volunteer to read the words on the board to the class in kindergarten. He is very good with words, and knows how to sound them out so the others in the class could follow along. He was glad to be able to help.

"Thank you," Bob says smiling. "Perhaps you could start with the most important one," he says looking over at the poster.

Colin leans forward and begins, "Our leaders empower employees to make our own choices and—"

"No, not that one," Bob interrupts. "The safety one."

"Oh. Right. Sure," Colin shuffles on the designer chair to stop that odd twinge in his lower back and reads loudly and clearly, the way he had been taught to. "Our employees' health and safety is our number one priority," he nods.

"Thanks Colin. That was great!" Bob smiles.

Colin smiles back and gives himself a tiny paw pump. "Yes," he says quietly. "Still got it."

"Perhaps George could read the next most important one for us?" Bob calls pointing at him with the marker.

George pushes his glasses up and leans forward, "The one about customers?"

"No, the one about freedom of choice," Bob

replies.

"Just being conscious of time," Harold coughs, unfolding himself from the chair. "Maybe you could take this up after?"

Graham agrees and makes a show of checking his watch. "Some of us have work to do."

"Can I go to the toilet?"

"What are you? Five?"

"I'm being polite."

"Let's take five minutes," sighs Harold as Bob pushes his thumbs into his temples.

"We've listened to what our employees said in our annual 'How you doin' survey," Harold cups his hand to his ear to demonstrate that he had listened, as everyone moves back to their seats.

Colin cups his hand to his ear, but can only hear George's stomach rumbling.

"And you said a lot of things," Harold continues sagely. "And we listened. Once we removed the profanity," he half smiles.

It's a smile that reminds Colin of the way Mrs Wombat would smile at her son Teddy when he would try to explain to her that the world was flat.

"We listened to your concerns about the annual review process, and made some important changes."

"About bloody time," Graham huffs and folds his arms tightly.

"Finally," Vanessa throws her hands up.

"The review process shouldn't be about focusing on your 'performance' as an employee," Harold begins, speaking as though it was somehow their fault that the annual review process was broken. "Over the last few years, it's unfortunately turned into a series of form-filling activities where some managers would focus less on their employees performance and more on playing favourites."

"I hate favouritism," Bob says, wiping some glaze from the corner of his mouth.

"The entire exercise would simply become people exaggerating what they had done through the year, or in a few unfortunate cases I'm not at liberty to discuss, actively sabotaging other's work to be able to rate higher and justify a bonus and a pay-rise," Harold voice trails off as he shakes his head slowly and sadly.

"We recognise that the review process should be a special event!" Harold suddenly yells, causing Colin to jump. "One celebrating your achievements!" he gives a hearty air punch as punctuation. "And for identifying the areas you can focus on to help you grow, to achieve *even more* next year."

"Oh," says Pooja looking around at the others. "This sounds like it could be good."

"You're right. This does sound promising," Umi says turning to Pooja. "I never liked how the rating I received effected my bonus, my pay review for next year, and long and short term any future promotional opportunities."

"Well, of course, it still does," says Harold. "But! We all know that money isn't everything," Harold joins his hands together and steeples his fingers. "I bet none of you come to work just for the money—"

"Put your hand down Graham," Bob calls without looking up.

"We all know that money is secondary to how you *feel* about your achievements."

"Bullshit!" George pretends to cough into his hand.

"Sorry George, did you have something to add?" Bob glares at him.

"Something in my throat," he waves his hand across his throat.

Colin raises a paw to cover his smile as George pretends to cough again.

"To cement that approach," Harold squints slowly over at George, "we have re-branded the name of the process. The term 'Performance' Review..." Harold makes air quotes with his fingers again.

He has quite dainty fingers for someone so tall, Colin thinks to himself. I wonder if he plays piano?

"...sounds very *negative*. As though we are somehow," he raises his dainty fingers again, 'assessing' your performance—"

"Uh. Isn't that exactly what you *are* doing?" George responds.

Harold ignores him and continues, "It's a process about helping you to *achieve*. So from today, we are pleased to announce that we are calling the system an..." he pauses dramatically. "*Achievement* Review!" he beams proudly and rocks slightly on the balls of his feet.

"What if you've got no achievements? Is it called a lack of achievement review?" Graham laughs loudly and slaps his thigh twice.

"We can talk about your personal circumstances offline Graham," Bob turns back to Harold. "Please go on..."

Colin can see the disappointment on Harold's face that everyone isn't as excited about the new name, so Colin sits up extra straight and puts on a big smile to show he's listening carefully.

Harold takes a deep breath, "As I was saying, this re-branding is driven from listening to our employees."

"If you're listening," Vanessa jumps in, folding her arms tightly, "then of course you've gotten rid of the High, Satisfactory, Low ratings that everyone hates?" she snorts and leans back in her chair smugly, looking around at the group. Gina laughs and mimes a 'mic drop.'

Harold studies Vanessa for a moment, as though he's been asked if water is wet. "Well, yes," he nods, "of course. As part of our assessment, we recognised that those ratings had the potential to... un-motivate our employees."

"Umm. Oh," Vanessa manages to squeeze out slowly, scratching her head.

Graham raises his hand slightly. "Are you happy with the term, 'un-motivate'?" Graham asks.

"Stop focusing on the wrong part of the story Graham," Bob quickly responds and drops his head. "It's like running a Kindergarten," he says softly to himself and presses his thumbs into his temples.

"If you're getting rid of things that are '*un*-motivating'," Graham continues. "Obviously the Bell Curve is going as well?" Graham laughs and slaps his knee to punctuate the comedy genius of his statement.

"Yes," Harold nods smugly again. "The company recognised the Bell Curve had the potential to appear inequitable. As such, we are no longer employing it as part of the process."

Colin watches Bob turn to Graham, ready to ask him to remain quiet, but for the first time since the day Colin started working there; Graham appears to have nothing to say.

"Oh that is good news," pipes up Bill. "Never liked the Bell Curve." He scoffs, shaking his head. "Always seemed unfair to me," he looks up toward the ceiling, reaching back into his memory. "Originally discovered in 1738 by the French mathematician Abraham de Moivre—"

"Childhood friend of yours?"

"Let's not get side-tracked," Bob jumps in, "Harold, please continue."

"That's fantastic," Alfred calls from the back of the room. "Now I'll get the rating I deserve, rather than being - 'bell-curved' - down."

"High's all round," George holds up a hand and hi-fives Umi.

"Yes," Harold continues, "as I was saying, we have removed the Bell Curve as a way to allocate and distribute achievement ratings. Instead, we are introducing the infinitely more fair..." he pauses dramatically again and looks out at the expectant faces. "Calibration sessions."

POP! Goes the tuft of fur on Colin's head.

Harold stands proudly, "The Calibration will occur during a discussion between Bob and his peers to ensure there is no favouritism."

"Who said there's favouritism?" Bob asks taking out another donut and mouthing 'thanks' to Umi.

"I'm pretty sure Harold's just said they don't trust you Bob," says Vanessa.

Harold adds quickly, "We're not saying we don't trust Bob. We're saying it's about keeping all decisions equitable." He continues to tell them that Bob and the other managers at his level will all get together and discuss the outcomes of the individual rankings and secure agreement of the final outcome.

"I thought you said we didn't have performance ratings anymore. What are they agreeing on?" Pooja scratches her head.

"The *Achievement rankings*." Harold says proudly and puffs out his chest.

"I'm sorry, the what now?" Graham leans forward.

"I thought he said they got rid of the shitty ratings?" Gina looks around at the others.

"That's correct," Harold smiles. "We have. We've replaced the..." he waves dismissively, "archaic High to Low Performance Rating system with a far more Agile 1 to 5 Achievement ranking."

"And here we go," Graham folds him arms and shakes his head.

Harold frowns, "It's designed in such a way that it

allows everyone to focus on their achievements."

"Hang on," Vanessa looks around at the others to confirm she isn't the only one confused... It turns out she isn't. "I thought when you started, you said this was about making things fairer for people by focusing on their individual performance—"

Harold raises his hand to stop her. "Not performance. Achievements," he corrects her slowly.

"Whatever..." Vanessa says. "But if it's supposedly only about *my* achievements," she folds her arms and leans back in the chair, "what is Bob 'calibrating' with other Managers?"

Harold nods slowly, "As I said, it's to ensure there is no favouritism. It's the step to calibrate the Achievement Ranking he believes you deserve, with other Managers at his level."

"Managers from other teams?"

"Yes," Harold confirms confidently. "And to ensure the process is completely impartial, the calibration sessions also include Managers from completely disparate functions as well."

Gina sucks a breath between her teeth. "Right," she hisses. "So, just to confirm we're all on the same page... what you're saying is that Managers who may have absolutely no idea what our department does; Managers who I've probably not even shared a lift with; and who most likely wouldn't give me the time of day if I gifted them my watch, are going to have a say about whether I deserve the rating that my direct manager, Bob, who I have worked with every day *all year*, has determined for me?"

"I'm not sure of your point?" Harold scratches his head.

Graham throws his hands in the air.

"What does it matter?" points out George. "There's no Bell Curve any more so It's not like they're fighting for anything. Everyone will get the ratings they deserve rather than worrying about whether their Boss is too much of a wimp to stand up for them in the meeting," he quickly glances over at Bob. "No offence. If we all do a great job, now we could all get a 'One'."

Harold smiles as though he's trying to explain quantum mechanics to a group of primary school children. "Yes. But of course, everyone can't receive an Achievement Ranking of 'One'. That's unrealistic. No team is going to have an entire team of level One achievers," he smiles down on the benevolently. "That's the benefit of the Calibration session, all the Managers will be able to agree alignment to the standard normal cumulative distribution."

"Did I get a concussion that I've forgotten about?" Vanessa asks, turning to Colin.

Colin looks at her head, concerned. "I can't see anything," he says and chews his bottom lip.

"Okay. So. This standard... normal..." Gina waves her hand trying to remember the whole term.

"cumulative distribution." Colin jumps in helpfully.

"...cumulative distribution..." she sighs, "is just a different name for 'Bell Curve', right?"

"As I said, we no longer have the Bell Curve." Harold folds his arms defensively. "Instead, we have the..."

"...Stupid boring cumulonimbus discombobulation." Graham chimes in. "Does this standard... whatever... happen to be shaped like a... bell, by any chance?"

"It's more like a mound—" Harold begins, miming a hill shape with his hands.

"Listen, "Vanessa jumps in. "It sounds to me like

I'm not only *still* competing against everyone else in my own team for my rating, now I'm at the mercy of some crutch-knuckle who's just heard my name for the first time."

"You can't say crutch-knuc—, you can't use that term Vanessa," Bob rubs his forehead. "And it's not a competition," he says, leaning forward. "The new system is very different."

Vanessa holds her hand up. "One," she counts off her on her fingers. "People are given a ranking. Two, 'Calibration' sessions order those ratings relative to other people's rankings. And three," she grabs her third finger. "Everyone is arranged from highest to lowest," she looks around at the rest of the room. "Yeah, I'm pretty sure that's the actual *definition* of a competition."

"Look. Let's not get side-tracked," Bob says quickly, "Continue Harold."

"May I please ask a clarifying question?" Bill asks, raising his hand.

"Oh God no," Bob rubs his forehead.

"Just so I'm clear," Bill sits upright. "You've done away with the unpopular three-tier High-Low

'Performance' rating, and the subsequent bell-curve process where my outcome is shoehorned into a predetermined number of ratings, based on an outdated and proven inaccurate model of statistical approximation..." Bill stops and raises his eyebrows.

Harold leans forward on the balls of his feet in anticipation. He glances over at Bob, who continues to rub his temples with his thumbs, then back to Bill. "I'm sorry, was there a quest—"

"... in preference to recognising," Bill continues as though there had been no pause, "an individual's actual performance against their agreed targets, and personal contribution to the company..."

"Uh..." Harold glances over at Bob again and coughs.

Bob shrugs in resignation and pushes his thumb a little bit further into his temple.

"Was... there a ques—" Harold leans forward even further in anticipation of the conclusion.

Colin moves back in his chair ready to yell, "TIM...BERRRR!"

"Then *my* manager," Bill starts up again, "would argue with other managers at a larger bell curve meeting, where my rating would be compared against other people across the company," he shakes his head and laughs, "some of whom are in roles so different to mine, there is little common ground between our contribution to the company, except for our pay grade. Making it all but impossible to be able to make any kind of accurate comparison..."

Harold opens his mouth again to ask if there's a question, then instead leans back and sucks in a breath.

"And we are replacing that with a 1 to 3 'Achievement' ranking, followed by a series of 'Calibration' sessions where individuals are 'balanced' into a 'standard normal cumulative distribution'?"

Colin wonders whether he has ever seen Bill make so many air quotes and notices that Bill's fingers aren't as dainty as Harold's.

There's a brief silence while Harold waits for Bill to continue. "Oh... are you? Okay. Sorry. Yes, that's correct."

Bill nods thoughtfully. "Well, that sounds splendid! Makes perfect sense, good job."

Harold beams. "Thank you!" he gives Bill a giant

thumbs up, then quickly turns back to Bill/ "Uh, that's it, you're done? Okay good. Yes. As I said, it's about listening to what our employees are saying and responding." Harold places a hand on Bob's shoulder, "You're lucky to have someone on your team who can distil concepts so succinctly. He must be a great asset."

Graham claps his hands on his thighs, "I reckon that just about wraps it up doesn't it?"

"Gosh I'm glad I wasn't here for the previous 'performance' review system," Colin says as they wait for the lift. "The new one Harold described sounds much fairer."

"They've just renamed it with newer wankier terms," Vanessa snorts, "Just another way to screw us out of what we deserve and make it sound like they're doing us a favour."

Colin moves forward and holds the lift door open for her and smiles, "You are well known for your cynicism though," he says playfully.

"Just because I'm cynical doesn't mean it's not

true," she smiles back as Bill slides in.

"This reminds me of the system they had in place—" Bill begins.

"Hold the lift!" Brenda calls, but doesn't walk any faster towards it.

Graham reaches out his arm and holds the door for her as Bill begins to talk at Vanessa.

"That's very polite of you Graham," Colin says stepping back for Brenda to get past into the lift. He knows it's good to acknowledge things like good manners.

"Yeah, I'm the salt of the Earth," he says to Colin stepping back into the corridor, "ask me any time. I'll tell you."

"What a waste of time," Brenda huffs as she steps past without saying thank you. "I don't have time for this. I'm far too busy. Let me tell you..." she talks at Vanessa and Bill, even though Bill is already speaking.

"You go ahead," Graham nods for Colin to step back out of the lift. "Forgot something," he smiles, "Can you give me a hand Colin?" he asks and let's go of the door as Colin steps back out.

"You bast—" Vanessa mouths as the doors clunk

closed.

"What did you forget?" Colin looks around to see if he can spot something.

"Forgot I said I'd stab myself if I ever got stuck in a lift again with Bill and Brenda," Graham laughs and waits until he's sure the lift has moved before pressing the button again.

That seems like an odd thing to forget, Colin thinks looking over at the fading 'The performance review system is changing. Check the intranet for more information. Review your performance! Develop into your career! Be the best you can be!" poster. "They'll need to update that to achievement," he points.

"Ha, that things been there for years. Every couple of years they rename it all to make it sound like they're doing something to help us. Nothing ever changes," he snorts. "We've had: Standard Deviation Variance, Gaussian Crescent, Performance Archway, Standard... complicated whatever this one is. It's all just another name for Bell-Curve. Which is just another name for shoehorning people into boxes."

"What do you mean boxes? I thought it was a curve?" Colin scratches his head

"You heard Harold, there's a 'Calibration' session to normalise the distribution into a hill-shaped outcome. The only reason for that is if there's a set number of 'achievement' rankings to fit everyone into."

"I'm confused," Colin says, confused. "Harold seemed quite certain that we were only being assessed on our own achievements."

"He also told George that not everyone can be a top performer. If everyone got a One because they outperformed their targets, everyone would expect a pay rise and a full bonus. They only have one pile of money to distribute across the entire company. So they can't afford to give everyone what they deserve," he snorts. "I know *that* from personal experience over the years." He peeks inside the lift as the doors slide open and holds the door for Colin when he's confirmed it's empty.

"I guess that... kind of... makes sense," Colin says jumping out of the way of the doors as they try to close on him.

"You can bust your gut and put in a super performance. But what happens when Harold and his crew has decided that there's only enough Ones available for our team to get one One?"

"One won?"

"One One," Graham holds up one finger.

"Oh. That's easy..." Colin replies, wondering now whether it is. "Wouldn't it go to the person on the team who was the best perform... er, achiever?"

"It would," Graham nods. "But what happens if Bob has *more* than one person who was the best achiever?"

"I don't understand," Colin scrunches his nose. "How can there be more than one best achiever?"

"You said it yourself," Graham continues, "you've worked hard this year. Exceeded your targets."

Colin nods and holds the door as they step into the corridor.

"And for putting in all that time; working late, extra stress, doing things over and above. You should be rewarded, right?"

"Right," Colin says, waving hi to Sergei as they walk past.

"Well, what if, while *you* outperformed what was expected of you, *I* also outperformed what was expected of me?"

Colin coughs to avoid saying, "That seems unlikely," and instead says, "I'm not sure of your point?"

"My point is, my furry compardre, is that because Bob has only one One rating to go 'round, he now has to choose whether you or I will receive that single; individual; One rating. And that means there's a 50% chance that you," he points at Colin... "get lumbered with a Two. Even though compared to what you were *supposed* to do, you shot the lights out."

Colin thinks hard for a moment, his tiny brow crinkling. "But Bob knows I... hypothetically, worked harder than you."

"Oh no no no, my fuzzy friend," Graham motions for them to step into a meeting room and picks up a marker. "It's not if I worked harder than *you*," he draws two circles on the whiteboard. "It's - if I worked harder than *I said I would.* If I know I can deliver 20 smaller projects in a year, but *said* I could only deliver ten," he scribbles '10' under the circle. "When I actually deliver the twenty I knew I could, I'm a super-star." He writes '20' and 'double', then draws smiley face inside the circle, "And would deserve a One."

Colin stares off into the middle distance as he taps his chin, "Following that logic, if I said I know I could deliver five really big projects and then worked really hard and delivered ten..."

Graham draws another circle and writes '5' and '10' and then 'double'. "Then you've also delivered twice as much as you were expected to, and therefore, would also deserve a One." Graham nods and draws a smiley face inside Colin's circle.

"But you said Bob only has one to give out?" Colin's voice trails off...

"Uh huh," Graham draws a sad face inside Colin's circle, and taps the marker onto the '20' on his side of the board. "And I've delivered twice as many projects as you, so..."

"But that's not fair!" Colin yells, "yours were easier!" he stamps his foot and crosses his arms tightly across his chest. He fumes for a second then remembers the entire conversation is hypothetical and calms back down. "But what about my extra work on top of my normal deliverables. Like 'stepping-up' and—"

"Old news," Graham shrugs and draws a line from left to right. "No-one remembers that." He writes 'last year' at the left end of the line, and today at the other. "Too much effort to review what happened back here," he draws a big question mark on the left-hand side. "Who can remember that far back? So mostly it's down to whether you were lucky enough to do something good in the last couple of weeks, or unlucky enough to screw something up. That's why I deliver all my work at the end of the year. When it means something." He taps the marker against the side of his head. "Up here for thinking," he says leaving a series of blue dots around his temple.

Colin frowns. It reminds him of the time in Mr Brownsnakes' drawing class. All year he had been enjoying himself making fun artwork. Mr Brownsnake even told him at the beginning of the year that one of his drawings was the best he had ever seen from a student Colin's age. All year he had topped the class, and then for the final assignment of the year, Mr Brownsnake's nephew Billy had done one good drawing, and Billy had won the award for Best Student. Even though Colin had been the best all year.

Colin didn't like to think badly of people, and Mr Brownsnake said it wasn't because Billy was his nephew, but...

"This is a big company, not school," he says to Graham. "I'm sure it will all work out fairly," he smiles uncertainly.

"Alright little bear," Bob begins, tapping a ream of paper on the table secretly pretending he's a newsreader. "Let's have a look at what you've been up to," he smiles over the table at Colin, "How do *you* think you've done this year?"

Colin scratches his head. He knows he's already sent Bob all his supporting documentation to show how much he had achieved. It contains all his targets and shows how he achieved more than he had been asked to. Surely everyone would say they have worked hard. And why did he say - *think* I've done. I know how I've done this year, Colin thinks to himself.

Colin sits up straight and talks about all the work he has delivered. He shows the graphs he has created to illustrate his targets and how he has exceeded them. There's a list of the new skills he's learnt and the ways he applied them to help increase efficiency and help others in the team.

Bob nods and makes a few positive noises to acknowledge what Colin is saying and taps a few new entries into his computer. "You've certainly been busy. I can see that according to your assessment, you've achieved your targets—"

"Exceeded!" Colin says bouncing up and down in his chair.

"Yes... Hmmm."

"Am I good enough for a 'One' Achievement Rating, Boss?"

"Hmm," Bob taps his chin. "Sometimes it's not just about exceeding your targets."

POP! Goes the tuft of fur on the top of Colin's head.

"Sorry about that Boss," he tries to push it back down. "I'm not sure what you mean?" Colin scratches his chin and wonders how doing better than was expected could be a bad thing. "I thought it was good to exceed my targets?"

"Well, yes," Bob crosses his legs and steeples his fingers slowly. "In most cases that's accurate. Sometimes though," Bob leans forward and gives Colin an awkward fatherly pat on the leg, "exceeding one or two of your targets means a person is putting in too much effort into those areas, at the expense of other targets. And we wouldn't be able to give a One ranking just based on exceeding some of the required targets."

Colin glances down at his leg and says, "But I've exceeded *all* of my targets." He looks back up at Bob. "So that means I can get a One Achievement Rating," he bounces in the chair again.

"Bob uncrosses and crosses his legs twice, and checks the computer and nods as though he's letting that information sink in. "Uh. It's certainly good progress, and it would set you up very strongly. Hmm," he says scrolling down the screen. "That's a great outcome for your day to day work. A person—"

Colin frowns.

"Or a... Koala, needs to do more than just what's assigned to them each day," he swings his fist through a long arc to make a self-conscious fist pump. "Being a

One means stepping up and taking on extra activities that benefit and add value for the company."

Colin smiles and grabs his Special Reminder Notebook. "I had wondered where all these extra achievements would fit in. I couldn't see where to put them on the form," he says and reads each one out loud, his chest puffing larger and larger with each achievement.

He talks about all the improvements he's made to the team's processes and procedures. The time he became Agile (capital A). When he helped run the series of meetings to find out why everyone thought they were spending too much time in meetings. Helping George be a team player in the team building session. Plus all the extra paperwork for Lacey from Legal and Sally from Safety that had needed to be completed.

"And don't forget the time I 'stepped up' into Brenda's role!"

"I'm not sure how much that actually counts for," Bob mumbles under his breath, then forces a smile. "Anything else?"

Colin flicks the page, "Oh, and the time you asked

me to take responsibility for completing your monthly reports."

Bob scratches his ear, "I don't remember asking you to complete my monthly reports?"

Colin squints down at his Special Reminder Notebook again. "Oh. No, you're right Boss. That' not until the next story. Sorry," he says flipping the page back.

"Yes," Bob nods and smiles. "A very good year indeed."

"And I've only been here 8 months!"

"Oh yes, that's right," Bob makes another note. "I'm not allowed to promise anything you understand, but you are certainly one of my top performers—"

"Achievers," Colin helpfully corrects him.

"Yes. Top achievers... in this team."

"Top enough to get a One?" Colin looks at him, eyes wide.

"Ha. You're a persistent little bugger," Bob laughs and nudges Colin's leg.

Colin glances at his leg and back to Bob.

"I'm not at liberty to discuss rankings, because they can change - either up or down - during the Calibration sessions," he leans forward and whispers conspiratorially, "But I can give you...," he looks around to check no-one else can hear him.

Colin checks under the table, in case anyone had been hiding under there before he and Bob had come into the meeting room.

"...an *indicative* rating." Bob whispers. Then quickly leans back and places one finger across his lips.

"*Indicative* is one of my favourite words," Colin smiles and swings his legs excitedly. "It's a fun word to say. I like the way it rolls off my tongue," he smiles and gazes off into the middle distance. "In-dicative," he says and looks back to Bob.

"That's good Colin. Well, as I say, this is only indicative—"

"Indicative."

"But as far as *I'm* concerned, you're definitely a One."

"I'm not supposed to say anything," Colin says quietly as he checks no-one is around and holds the door open as they step into the coffee shop.

Graham squints down at him. "Then you probably shouldn't," he says and places his plastic re-usable coffee cup that reads, 'If I arrive late, it's important I make up for it by leaving early' onto the counter. "Long black - but not too long - thanks mate."

"And I'll have a cappuccino please," Colin reaches up and places his green re-usable coffee cup next to Graham's.

"What's the name?" the lady with the purple hair, who serves Colin every day, asks.

Colin wonders how many Koalas the coffee shop gets as customers and says slowly and carefully, "Co-lin." He turns back to Graham as they step away from the counter. "Bob told me I'm doing a great job, and everyone is very pleased with my work."

Colin smiles and steps to one side for a nice lady in a grey three-piece suit carrying an expensive leather briefcase and a chainsaw. She smiles back before ordering a flat white.

"Hey! That's great buddy. Well done!" Graham smiles and claps him on the back.

Colin grins and kicks the ground softly. "Oh, stop

it," he grins sheepishly. "Anyway," he whispers, looking around quickly. "What I'm not supposed to tell anyone is that..." he lifts his hand up to his mouth and whispers, "he's told me he is going to give me a..." Colin checks again to make sure no-one can hear, "a One!" he smiles from ear to ear. "I knew all my hard work would pay off. Even though I just did it to be the best employee I could be and add value to the company," he folds him arms and nods. "It's nice to be recognised though."

"Coffee for Caylen!" the purple-haired waitress calls as she pushes the green re-usable cup on the bench.

"Colin?" Colin leans toward the counter and raises an eyebrow.

"Says Caylen," she says checking the name she had written on the docket.

Graham reaches forward and grabs both cups. "He *told you* that you would get a One?"

"Shhh!" Colin says waving his paws downwards.

Graham leans against the door to hold it open and slides out of the way of the lady in the suit who is now carrying the chainsaw and briefcase in one hand. "He shouldn't have told you that."

"I know, I know," Colin takes a sip of his coffee and reaches up to push the crossing button. "But I was being a," he laughs, "a 'persistent little bugger'."

"I don't know how to break this to you little buddy, but he..." Graham looks up at the clouds passing overhead, casting a shadow, "But he... kind of says that to everyone," he adds quickly, "he shouldn't have told you because it's not locked in," he shakes his head strongly. "I don't want to rain on your parade mate," he looks down at Colin, "because if anyone deserves it, it's you."

"Oh, I know it's only indicative," Colin smiles and looks off to the side, "In-*dicative*," he giggles, *"indica-*tive," he smiles and turns back to Graham. "But I showed how I had exceeded all my targets, and took responsibility for extra work, like stepping up into Brenda's role—"

"I'm not sure that will account for much."

"And all the other extra activities,'" he says swiping his card through the security gate. "I've clearly achieved more than I needed to," he pauses, "and I've only been here 8 months!"

"I've got the results of the calibration session Colin. So I'm able to give you your final rating for the year," Bob says leaning forward in the chair.

Colin leans forward so far on his chair, swinging his legs excitedly, he nearly falls off. 'One, one, one,' he chants in his head.

"I'm pleased to tell you," Bob pauses. "After calibrating your achievements with the other Managers in different functions, I'm pleased to tell you..."

"Yes?"

Bob smiles broadly, "You ended up as a very, very strong..." he double checks his notes. Two," Bob smiles proudly and raises his hand to give Colin a high-five.

"Two?" Colin's legs stop swinging.

"A very, very *strong* Two," Bob declares and punches the air. "*Almost* a 'One'."

"But, a... Two." Colin slumps, unable to hide his disappointment. He knows he has worked hard and achieved lots more than he needed to.

"Yes," Bob punches the air again. This time with less gusto. "A really high Two. Any more of a Two and it would have been a One. You should be proud of yourself. Almost a 'One' is very difficult to achieve."

"But I thought I'd done really well," Colin scratches his head frowning. "I've exceeded all my targets, and only been here 8 months."

Bob leans in closer to Colin. "You did, you did," he says. "And I fought hard for you in those Calibration sessions," he says sincerely, not mentioning the one he forgot to attend. "It's just that all the other Managers felt that it would be unfair to give you a 'One', because you've only been here for eight months," Bob sits back and shakes his head as though it's the first time he's heard this news. "They felt it wouldn't be fair to others who had been here for the full year." He straightens up and smiles broadly. "But don't worry. Next year things will be different. You'll have a full year under your belt... uh, do you wear a belt?"

"But I achieved more than a year's worth of my targets in less than a year..." Colin tilts his head in confusion, "Shouldn't that make it... better?"

"I agree, but there's only limited numbers of 'Ones'

to go around," he looks down at his notes," and virtually all of them went to Sales, because they bring in our revenue."

"I don't understand why my achievements would be compared to people in completely different functions?" Colin scratches his head.

"That's the system unfortunately," Bob stands up to show that the meeting is over. "We've all got the same problem. I get compared against managers who run teams that are very different to what we do here."

"But, that kind of makes sense," Colin says. "Even though the team is different, you're all still doing the same job... managing a team to get the best from them," Colin notes.

Bob stares for a moment then slowly turns towards the door. "I wish it were that straightforward," he shrugs, ignore the fact that it is. "As I say, you should be very proud of your performance."

"Achievements," Colin says flatly and slides slowly off the chair.

"You should be very pleased with your strong, *strong* Two," he says, patting Colin on the shoulder. "You've done a great job." He looks up and sees

Graham appear from the lift and walking towards them. "As opposed to *some people*," Bob mutters.

"Okay," Colin says slowly, his gaze dropping back to the floor. "Thanks Boss," he sighs. "I guess."

"And there's more good news!" Bob beams excitedly. "After you told me about how Brenda spends most of her time waiting to deal with 'urgent requests' I had a conversation with Harold, so it looks like there might be an opportunity to expand your role to take on some of Brenda's work."

'I wonder if that means she is getting promoted?' thinks Colin. "Wait, why me Boss? I thought I was only stepping up that one time?"

"That's what makes me a good manager," Bob says and turns away from the approaching Graham. "I saw you had included Brenda's job in your Career Development Plan," he says and begins walking down the corridor. "I'll admit I was surprised," he calls back over his shoulder. "I'd thought you had found it a bit hectic, but I'm happy to help you grow in your career."

Colin tries to say that he only put it on his Career Development Plan because Bob had told him to... because it would look good at Performance Review time, but isn't able to get the words out before Bob disappears around the corner.

He doesn't think he'd like the idea of dealing with the stress of 'Urgent Requests' dropping out of the sky as a permanent job.

"How'd you go?" asks Graham.

Colin blinks a few times and slowly smiles. He lifts himself back up, pulls his shoulders back and holds his head high. "I'm a very high Two," he nods strongly. "Almost a One," he smiles. "It's like Harold told us - It's our *own* Achievement rating, it's not a competition against others," he closes his paw and fist-pumps the air. "It's a competition against *ourselves.* Bob is going to give me a couple of Improvement Opportunities that I can work on, so I can be even better next year."

"Uh. You've done pretty good this year mate. There's no way you shouldn't have been a One," Graham shakes his head, "Come grab a coffee."

"Oh, Bob said he was very pleased with my work," waving a 'no time' to Graham. "It wasn't because I hadn't *achieved.* He couldn't get the others in the calibration session to agree to his rating, because I hadn't been here a full year."

"Sorry buddy, that's such bullshit," Graham frowns.

"That's okay," Colin smiles. "When the next review comes around, I'll have my year up and I'll be on the train straight to One town," he beams, mimicking the wheels of a train turning. "Did you get a One?"

"A One? Ha! No way I'm ever going to get a One. They don't give you a One unless you're a massive suck-up."

Colin frowns and decides not to pursue that line of thought for the moment.

"Anyway, yeah you did better than me mate. I got a bit of a caning. Low Two. No idea why," he shrugs, almost dropping his plastic re-usable cup that reads, 'My Boss is a useless c*nt'. "I'm used to it though. That's the price you pay for telling it like it is."

"I've been robbed!" Brenda appears around the corner muttering to herself as much as anyone else.

Colin quickly spins around to see if he can catch the robber. "I've only got little legs, but if I see him, I can bite his ankles."

Brenda stops and crosses her arms so tightly; Colin is worried she is going to crush her own ribs.

"Ridiculous," she snorts. "Absolutely unreasonable.

I think it's discrimination," she wags her finger sternly. "He told me I would have got a *Three* if that Graduate hadn't set fire to the photocopier."

"Twice," Colin corrects her.

Graham slowly holds up three fingers.

"Really?" Colin asks open mouthed.

"It's outrageous!" Brenda says to a confused woman just walking past.

Colin looks up at Brenda. "Um, Brenda. When you say you were *almost* a Three..." he pauses and swallows. "Are you saying... does that mean you... you got a..." he takes a breath. "Do you mind if I ask what you did get?"

"I don't mind at all. People need to know about the injustice," she snorts angrily. He gave me a Two," she shakes her head in disbelief. "Can you believe that?"

"I can't believe you got a Two," Graham says.

"And apparently a *low* Two," Brenda clenches her jaw. "The people here are so ungrateful. Don't they understand how important I am in keeping this company running. Do you know how much work I have to do?" she snorts. "No-one cares."

"You got that right," Graham mutters. "Anyway,"

he stands straight. "Some of us have work to do," he says and turns towards the lifts. "You want me to bring you one back?" he holds up his cup.

Colin waves a 'no thanks' as Brenda continues to tell him how busy she is, but her voice fades away as Colin eyes glaze over.

All he can think is that while Bob said Brenda was low, and he was high... But there is no low and high. They are both - Two. If anyone looks at the ratings of the team, all they will see is - Colin, Graham and Brenda, are all performing— achieving, at the same level... Two.

"I need to get back to work," Colin mumbles.

" *You* need to get back to work? How do you think I feel with how overloaded I am..."

Colin the Koala drags his feet slowly back to his desk. He thinks about the nights preparing for his review. Staying up late, drinking coffee to stay alert, documenting his achievements in his Special Reminder Notebook. He looks back over his shoulder at Brenda, who is complaining at a startled Bill, who had unluckily walked around the corner to pick up some printing and been ambushed.

Colin climbs up onto his 'your safety and comfort is our number one priority' chair, slides forward, pushes himself back up and feels himself slide forward again. He tries unsuccessfully to get comfortable while he ponders all the extra time he has put in. All the extra hours he has spent working at home. Bouncing ideas and strategies off his friends, even when they would tell him to stop worrying about it and have another beer. He moves his mouse to bring up the login screen and hears Brenda still talking behind him.

Colin the Koala reaches forward towards the keyboard, pauses and instead picks up his green re-usable coffee cup.

"Hang on Graham," he calls and then says softly, grinding his teeth. "Maybe I do have time for coffee after all."

"I want to know who received our 'One'," Graham says sipping his long - but not too long – black coffee. "No-one deserves it more than you do," he says, motioning with his cup towards Colin. "And if it wasn't you, it clearly should have been me," he shakes his head angrily. "Such bullshit," he turns back to Colin and holds his fingers up, a tiny gap between the tips of his thumb and index finger. "A bee's dick away from a 'Three'," he snorts. "Can you believe that?"

Colin opens his mouth, then quickly closes it again.

"Coffee for Kola!" the barista with the shirt that says Barry on it, calls, pushing Colin's cup forward.

"Colin?" Colin leans forward hopefully.

The barista glances down at his note, "Says Kola."

Graham reaches over the counter. "I've got it for you mate. Let's go."

"Have a good one," the barista calls to them as they walk back outside.

"You too mate," says Graham.

"See you later Barry," calls Colin and grabs the door handle. "Keep the noise out for you," he says and pulls the door firmly closed.

"Yeah, thanks Kola, or maybe, was it Colin?" the barista says, turning off the coffee machine.

ELWOOD SCOTT

Acknowledgements

It's taken a few years to finally get Colin to this point.

Firstly, thank you to Mitch Pleasance for the amazing job of creating the illustration of Colin. Mitch is also the guy who did my typewriter tattoo. If you're looking for a good tattoo, Mitch Pleasance is your man. You can find him on Instagram - @mitchpleasance

Thank you to everyone who read, reviewed and provided useful and beneficial feedback. It has all made a difference to how this book turned out. Also, thank you for not rolling your eyes every time I'd stop in the middle of a conversation and say, "Wait. I need to write that down. That's going in the book."

Louise, thank you for your many scribbled comments, edits, feedback and support. And also for your sage advice to not keep all my horses in one bucket.

Annabel for your constant laughter, support and ongoing astonishment that baristas can get the name 'Colin' so wrong, so regularly, and in so many ways.

My podcast buddy Scott for being a sounding board, providing advice and support on content and on the cover design. And for helping to build my social media presence, despite my inconsistent involvement.

Thanks Liam for the cover idea, Miranda for the suggestion to make Colin a Koala, and all the people who gave me ideas (and by ideas, I mean – actual events that most of these stories are based on- or would be if they weren't all fictional like my lawyer says: Jerzy, Eb, Liam, Mick, Connor, and of course my own previous bosses and team-mates.

Thanks to Psychostick, Kiss, Alice Cooper, Anvil and Mushroomhead for the background music while I was writing.

And thank you to all the people who were there in the beginning who helped to shape Colin into the Koala he is today.

I hope you've enjoyed reading about my adventures, and that you can join me for some others in Book Two – Colin Keeps Working.

Other stories in the Colin the Koala series:

- 🐾 Colin the Koala works remotely.
- 🐾 Colin the Koala learns Continuous Improvement.
- 🐾 Colin the Koala goes to work drinks.
- 🐾 Colin the Koala takes part in a Group Project.
- 🐾 ~~Colin the Koala kills a co-worker.~~ (no longer available).
- 🐾 Colin the Koala Fails Fast.
- 🐾 Colin the Koala gets Flexible.
- 🐾 And (unfortunately) there's many more...

Thank You!

Thank you for reading **Colin Calls the Help Desk.**

I hope you have enjoyed the stories as much as I enjoyed writing them.

If you did; please drop a review, because it will help me out.

If you enjoy typing website addresses, all you need to do is type the below into your browser and it will take you straight there:

https://www.amazon.com/review/create-review?&asin= 0645052426

Otherwise, just jump to the book page on Amazon and scroll down.

You're a legend!

Cheers

Elwood

Printed in Great Britain
by Amazon